Body Conscious

by

Ana Diamond

This is a work of fiction. Names, characters, places, and incidents are either the product of the author's imagination or are used fictitiously, and any resemblance to actual persons living or dead, business establishments, events, or locales, is entirely coincidental.

Body Conscious

Cover Art by *Kristian Norris*

The Wild Rose Press, Inc.
PO Box 708
Adams Basin, NY 14410-0708
Visit us at www.thewildrosepress.com

Publishing History
First Edition, 2021
Trade Paperback ISBN 978-1-5092-3687-9
Digital ISBN 978-1-5092-3688-6

Published in the United States of America

"That's Detective James Rivers," Abrams said. "He came all the way up from New York City to our little town in the beautiful and scenic Hudson Valley. He'll be the lead investigator on this case since I know you ladies will be frequent callers."

"Let's be clear, I've never called you," Lily said. "It's always been Shanna."

Abrams gave her a coy smile. He seemed flattered by the idea.

"Nice to meet you, Detective Rivers," Lily said, finally turning toward the man who approached them.

Her breath caught in her throat. She didn't know what she had been expecting, but not him—not that angelic face with large sky-blue eyes, pronounced cheekbones, and silken black hair. The only part of him that matched her ideas of what detectives looked like were his tattooed arms—she should know, as her dad had been a cop.

May he rest in peace.

But the tattoos on James's shoulders could not be considered *subtle*. Snakes slid down his arms, past his rolled-up shirtsleeves, coiling around his biceps and thick forearms. One corner of his mouth lifted as he caught her staring.

Praise for Ana Diamond

Body Conscious was a finalist in the 2020 Tara Contest.

Chapter One

"Lily, can you go down and check on the new body? The last thing I need is a decomposing corpse."

Lily Reynolds sucked in a frustrated breath at her older sister Shanna's yell from the Reynolds Funeral Home embalming room.

Zachary strikes again.

"All right."

Her twenty-year-old brother, Zachary, often forgot to secure the latch on the refrigerator doors after he pushed the recently deceased into the compartment. It was a critical mistake no one wanted to explain to the dead person's family. But Lily didn't understand what was difficult about doing it right the first time. Zachary had worked at the family business for almost five years—the same length of time as her. One would think the importance of the simple task would sink into that thick skull.

Now, she had to stop applying lipstick to Mrs. Klein whose viewing was scheduled to start in one hour and go downstairs to check on the refrigerator.

She pulled off her latex gloves and made her way down to the basement level, where Antonio, their hearse driver, usually pulled in with Zachary in the shotgun seat and their newly acquired client in the back. Upon arrival, the client was inserted into an individual horizontal refrigerator for preservation until it was time

1

for embalming and then a makeover by Lily.

At the bottom of the stairs, she flicked on the fluorescent lights and didn't see the black hearse. That meant Zach was with Antonio, probably picking up another client. It had been a busy week at the funeral home—not a complaint. She liked her job. She got to perform a service for the loved one's family and be creative at the same time.

What's not to like?

She turned left to walk to the towering refrigerators lined up against the wall and then stopped. The body of a man she'd never seen before lay on the floor in a large pool of blood. Heart pounding hard inside her chest, a loud squeal escaped her lips.

"Are you okay?" Shanna yelled from the top of the stairs.

"It's a body!"

"There are lots of bodies down there."

"This one's not one of ours!"

Shanna barreled down the stairs, stopped, and bent her rail-thin body over at the waist to look closer at their visitor.

"Gunshot wound," Lily said, pointing at the man's head. "See it, near the left temple?"

"I see it. I see it."

Lily didn't cringe—she dealt with death all day long, but she'd never been in a potential crime scene. Usually, the bodies came to her with their affairs already settled. Her job was to make them presentable for the families, not to figure out why they died.

Looking down at the poor man's contorted limbs made her want to gather him up in their linens and give him the full Reynolds treatment. She leaned over, intending to pull down and straighten his faded red T-shirt.

"No! You can't touch anything." Shanna's hands shot out. "It's a crime scene."

"Geez, all right. I just feel bad for the guy. How do you know he didn't do this to himself?"

"You think he wandered in when the garage door was open and decided to do it here? Why would he do that? Plus, I don't see a gun near the body. That makes me think it's less likely a suicide and more likely a crime." Shanna pulled out her cell phone and dialed the local precinct. "We need to call the cops. I'll ask for Don Abrams. He's the only real detective in this minuscule town."

Lily didn't find it unusual that her sister had the local precinct's number stored in her phone. Shanna's nosy nature meant she asked more questions about their clients than seemed appropriate. But Detective Donald Abrams, who had a thing for her sister, didn't mind. So it didn't surprise Lily when a quick chat on the phone led to Abrams coming over with a full entourage of crime scene investigators.

"You ladies certainly aren't boring," Detective Abrams said, towering over the two of them and rubbing at his whiskered stubble. "The last time I was called here, you thought a body had been stolen right from under you when actually the poor soul was just misplaced."

Shanna fisted both hands on her hips. "I didn't *misplace* Mr. Daniels. I simply forgot I had already put him in the casket for the viewing. And what a beauty his casket was—gorgeous cherry wood with a high shine finish."

"Can we focus on the new guy?" Lily snapped. "There's clearly been a murder."

"Pipe down there, firecracker. I don't need you scaring off my new recruit." Abrams waved to a man standing across the room.

Although it was unusual for her, Lily did not react to Abrams's comment. Her fiery red hair automatically generated unwanted comments about her assertive personality. She didn't feel the need to add more to that bucket.

"That's Detective James Rivers," Abrams said. "He came all the way up from New York City to our little town in the scenic Hudson Valley. He'll be the lead investigator on this case since I know you ladies will be frequent callers."

"Let's be clear, I've never called you," Lily said. "It's always been Shanna."

Abrams gave her a coy smile. He seemed flattered by the idea.

"Nice to meet you, Detective Rivers," Lily said, finally turning toward the man who approached them.

Her breath caught in her throat. She didn't know what she had been expecting, but not this—the angelic face with large sky-blue eyes, pronounced cheekbones, and silken black hair. The only part that matched her ideas of what detectives looked like were his tattooed arms. She should know; her dad had been a cop.

May he rest in peace.

But the tattoos on James's shoulders could not be considered *subtle*. Snakes slid up his arms, past his rolled-up shirtsleeves, coiling around his thick forearms and biceps. One corner of his mouth lifted as he caught her staring.

"You must be Lily." He stuck out one hand for her to shake. "Detective Abrams told me so much about you and your sister on the way over."

She reciprocated and let his warm hand envelop hers. She hadn't expected to like it. But in fact, holding his hand made her feel safe and happy. If he felt her pulse, he would know her heart had sped up. Despite her body's reaction, Lily immediately wanted to pull her hand away. She wasn't into cops—or rather, she *refused* to be into them. They were nothing but trouble. Her parents had been killed by an escaped prisoner seeking revenge against the cop who caught him. Her father was that cop. She wanted nothing to do with that life ever again.

She released his hand. "I came down to make sure our brother Zachary closed the refrigerators correctly. That's when I found the body." Her voice came out louder than usual—a sign she felt self-conscious.

"Do either of you know the victim?"

Lily shook her head; Shanna did the same.

"Who else was in the house when the body was found?" he asked.

"Just Shanna and me. Zachary and Antonio, the hearse driver, had gone out again for client retrieval."

"Shanna," James asked. "Did you see or hear anything out of the ordinary?"

"I heard Lily scream and ran down to the basement from the embalming room. I didn't hear anything out of the ordinary before that."

"Do either of you know anyone who might have a reason to dump a body in your place of business?"

Again, they each shook their heads.

Chuckling, Abrams took a step forward. "Don't be

nervous. He's not interrogating you—yet."

"Very funny, Don," Shanna told him. "You know we had nothing to do with this."

"Maybe, but this is a crime scene. We have to follow procedure. I'm sorry, but you were the first at the scene," he replied, looking straight at Lily.

James poked an elbow at Abrams. "I got this."

Abrams stared at him for what felt like an eternity, then walked toward the crime scene investigators bagging evidence.

Not losing a step, Rivers continued. "Do either of you have any enemies?"

"Who doesn't have enemies?" Lily replied.

"What Lily means, Detective," Shanna said, "is who doesn't know people who might be a little jealous? But certainly, not enemies. No, sir."

Lily's brain stopped working the moment she'd laid eyes on James Rivers, but her sister—who clearly watched too many crime shows on TV—was taking this to another level.

"People who are jealous?" he asked.

"Envious. That's more accurate." Shanna fiddled with her blonde hair. "After all, business is booming. We have a long tradition here. Our customers trust us."

"And the two of you own this funeral parlor?"

"Yes. Our mom left it to us. She inherited it from her family. Zachary, our brother, is also a co-owner, but he's not here at the moment. We're morticians."

James's eyes went straight to Lily's. "Morticians? You mean you dress up dead bodies?"

Lily cleared her throat. It wasn't the first time she'd been judged by her job—pretty much everyone did. In fact, most people stayed away from her. The idea that she voluntarily spent her day with the dead hadn't fostered lasting friendships—or romantic relationships, for that matter.

Sticking out her chin, she snapped, "We provide funeral services to people who've lost their loved ones." She was proud of what she did and had no problem showing it.

James raised his hands up in surrender. "I meant no offense. It surprises me that a beautiful woman like you would be interested in such a morbid field."

Lily glanced at Shanna whose jaw had dropped.

"I mean—that's not what I meant." James stumbled on his words.

Lily looked down at her feet. Her ears burned from embarrassment. She wanted to flee from the scene.

"Don't worry, I won't keep you much longer," he said. "I know this must be difficult. We can keep the facility under surveillance while the investigation continues."

She nodded at his quick save. He was a cop, after all, tasked with protecting the public.

"James, we got ID," Abrams announced from the spot where he crouched near the body. One of the investigators, with gloved hands, looked inside the victim's wallet, pulled something out, and handed it to Abrams.

"Michael Ronan," Don said. "Ring a bell for either of you?"

"No, we've never heard of him," Lily replied.

"All right. Bag him up," Abrams said. "Let's get the scene ready for evidence collection and cleaning."

After preparations for removal of the body were underway, Abrams came back to them. "All set here?"

"Yeah, I think I've got everything I need." James went back to sounding official.

"Great. I'll meet you back in the car. Ladies, the crime scene investigators will stick around to collect all the evidence. Thank you for your cooperation." Abrams tipped his head at them and walked toward the exit.

The awkward silence that followed made Lily cringe, but she was used to it. People often judged what she did for a living, especially men. They expected her to work at Mona's Flower Shop or Sweet Teeth, the local bakery. But she loved her job and no cop was going to make her feel otherwise.

Finally, Shanna broke the silence. "I need to finish up Mr. Zhang's embalming, and you need to get Mrs. Klein ready for her viewing. I'm sure Detective Rivers understands and won't take up much more of our time."

He nodded. "Certainly. Please, call me James."

"I'll see you soon." Shanna squeezed Lily's arm and headed back upstairs.

Lily felt her skin heat. James had simultaneously insulted and complimented her, yet she didn't walk away. There was something…different about him.

"Listen, sorry about my insensitive comment. I wasn't thinking."

"I get it all the time—I mean, the morbid part."

"I'm sure you get the beautiful part, too."

Lily smiled and shook her head. Maybe he couldn't help himself. "Shanna's right. I've got to get back to work. Mrs. Klein needs some lipstick before her viewing. Thanks for coming out so quickly. We've never been involved in anything like this. I hope you catch the killer."

"I may have a few more questions to ask while the

case progresses," he murmured.

Lily turned. "Am I under suspicion?"

"Not that I'm aware of."

"That's good to hear. I'm happy to help, anytime." She returned a wicked smile—the kind that always got her into trouble.

James seemed stunned into silence. That was her cue to leave. He could find his own way out. She walked back up the stairs toward the makeup room, not looking back. She put up a confident front, but her stomach roiled at the thought that Detective James Rivers might contact her about the crime she'd stumbled upon.

The idea that she might be implicated disgusted her. Even though her father was a cop for more than twenty years before he'd been murdered, he'd never discussed the gruesome stuff he saw in the field when he came home. Being part of a criminal investigation was not something she was familiar with. Neither was finding a random body on her basement floor.

But she didn't want to worry too much about James's investigation. Abrams had said he was new, and she had to believe that would help her on some level. She wasn't guilty, but the investigation in her place of business made her a bit twitchy.

Lily took in a deep, cleansing breath as she replaced her latex gloves. Her hands shook.

Everything is going to be okay.

She picked up the mauve-toned lipstick that Mrs. Klein's family had provided and began applying it to the old woman's lips. Her shoulders relaxed. Work did that for her, so that was what she would do, drown herself in work.

Hopefully, that would keep out those pesky thoughts of murder and James Rivers's perfect biceps.

****

James rubbed his weary eyes. He'd been sitting at his desk, analyzing the case through the night but had not found any solid leads.

"Long night?" Don Abrams asked as he popped a doughnut hole in his mouth. "I'd offer you one of these, but I'd have to go over to Sammy's desk to get it. That's mean I'd have to listen to him complain about his mother-in-law again."

James chuckled, then yawned. "No worries. This case is making me too anxious to eat."

"Why? You're finally getting somewhere with Lily Reynolds?"

"She's not a suspect, Don. I can't bring her in without evidence."

"I know that, but she found the body. And why was it there in the first place? There's got to be some connection."

"I don't think there is. They called us, remember? She could've easily disposed of the body in a funeral home."

"She probably didn't mean to kill the guy. I doubt she's some serial killer. It could've been a crime of passion. Calling us makes her look innocent."

James frowned. There was nothing about Lily Reynolds that screamed crime of passion. In fact, her reaction to a possible murder in her own basement seemed fairly normal—even for a mortician.

James pointed his pen at Abrams. "Where's the gun? No gun was found at the scene. Someone dumped the body."

"She had the sense to get rid of it."

"Finding a dead body in your place of business—that isn't supposed to be there—doesn't look good, I'll give you that, but the suspicion ends there."

James watched Abrams take in a frustrated breath and lean against the file cabinet. He might be pissing off a senior officer, but he wanted to do things the right way—by the book.

"Did the forensics come back yet?" Abrams asked.

"It did." James pulled the report out from a folder on his desk.

Abrams took it. "Why didn't you say so?"

"It doesn't change anything."

He watched Abrams scan the document. "The victim was found lying in his own blood, but no spatter was found around the body which indicates he was placed in the facility after his death."

"So he was dumped by an outside party," James said with a nod.

Abrams glared at James. Then went back to reading the document. "No fingerprints were found on or near the body." He turned the page over. "A powder-like substance was identified on the left collar of the victim's shirt. Analysis revealed the powder to be cosmetic in origin." He pursed his lips. "What more do you need?"

"He could've picked that up from anywhere. A girlfriend. His mom—"

"A funeral home."

"I'm not saying it's impossible, but it's a stretch." James's stomach ached. He didn't want it to be Lily, but he couldn't deny how it looked.

"Isn't she the one who applies the makeup to

the…dearly departed?"

James shrugged. "You know them better than I." He knew his behavior was unprofessional, but he couldn't help his frustration. "Why are you so interested in pointing the finger at her? I haven't found anything on this Michael Ronan yet, and we haven't even had a chance to speak to anyone related to him. Plus, we need to talk to Zachary. He's a young man probably up to no good."

"You can look into the whole family. In fact, you should. Look, I know she's attractive. I went out with Shanna a few times, but that doesn't keep me from doing my job. I've had an almost perfect career in investigations. I'm not going to let this case ruin my track record. When I know I'm right, I go after it."

"This time, you've got it wrong, Don. I'm not interested in her on a personal level. First of all, I take my job very seriously. Second, your track record will be ruined if you continue on the Lily Reynolds trail."

"I know you take your job seriously, but I have way more experience and seniority than you. Trust me; I know what I'm talking about."

James knew better than to push his boss too hard. He would have to appease him by going through the motions and finding the real killer. For now, he would change the subject. Eventually, the truth would come out. It always did.

He looked at his chief. "Pretty quiet out there on the floor today. I remember in the City, the phones would ring nonstop day after day."

Abrams grunted. "Yeah, welcome to Manorview."

"Anyway, to your last point about Lily, I have no interest in dating. At least, not for a very long time."

Abrams scoffed. "That's very dramatic. Are you a member of the Broken Hearts Club?"

"I'm the president. That's all I'll say about that. What happened between you and Shanna?" James asked, purposely diverting the conversation.

"Nothing. We dated, but I'm not the marrying type, and she wants to get married. It's that simple. But we still see each other off and on. Nothing too serious."

"Sounds like you two aren't right for each other but can't stay away."

"It's complicated. We have a history that's hard to shake. But I also have a job to do first and foremost."

"Gonna get sticky if you're pointing the finger at her sister."

"Ha. I'm being thorough. I think she understands that. Look, she called me, remember?"

"It's a twisted game you play."

"It's a two-way street. Maybe one day you'll understand."

"No, thanks. I'm done with including anyone I care about in this lifestyle. Too dangerous."

Abrams craned his neck to make eye contact. "Someone got hurt?"

James looked away from his superior. Once the floodgates opened and his emotions bubbled up to the surface, it would be difficult to stop.

"Say no more. I get it. This life isn't for everyone. I personally try not to get too deep."

"So you have a wall up? That makes sense."

"Call it what you want, but for me, the job comes first, and I suggest you start thinking that way if you want to get anywhere. Over the years, I've had several officers quit, but I think you've got potential, and I'd hate to see you go down that road."

"I appreciate the advice, but I'm not sure I'm made from that cloth."

Abrams's hands went up in surrender. "It's your choice. You'll learn the hard way."

"Not if I hang around you too much."

"Then there's still hope for you."

"Great."

"You should pull the funeral home's records. See if there's a connection with our victim, Michael Ronan."

"I already have."

"And?"

"There's nothing except a few complaints from a customer."

Abrams straightened. "What kind of complaint?"

"Someone by the name Taylor." James rifled through the transcribed telephone notes. "Sarah Taylor. On March fifth of this year, she called the funeral home, all upset that she had not been provided the services she paid for. She claimed her mother's makeup was not done to her specifications, and the food and beverages served were also not what she had requested. The telephone note indicates Sarah kept screaming into the receiver and would not calm down. Lily finally hung up on her."

"Uh-huh. Is that it?" Abrams asked, rubbing at his whiskers.

"An hour later, the same Sarah called again to say she was going to report them to the state and get all of their licenses revoked. Then she hung up."

"Who wrote these telephone notes?"

"Lily Reynolds."

"Can we link Sarah to Michael Ronan?"

"Not without my calling Sarah to find out."

"Do it, and if there is a link, bring Lily in for questioning." Abrams turned to leave the office.

"Abrams."

He stopped short of the doorway.

"She didn't do it."

"How do you know?"

"Gut feeling."

"You know that won't hold any water."

"There's no way she did it. Impossible."

"Prove it."

James watched Abrams leave his office. In the short time he'd lived in Manorview, he'd heard all the office talk about the legendary Detective Abrams. He learned that over the man's long career, his track record had been almost perfect in solving crimes. Eventually, he'd been recruited to Manorview for a top dog position in a cushy, friendly neighborhood. You could call that selling out, but people got older, and no one wanted to be in the trenches forever.

James wanted to please Abrams. He wanted to impress him. It would help his career in the long run, but he also couldn't deny his instincts. Despite being the newbie in town, he had damn good instincts. Homicide was relatively new to him, but when he was right about a case, he genuinely felt it in his bones—a natural instinct.

His dad used to tell him that all the time, "James, I know you'll make something of yourself. You've got brains and more common sense than anyone I know."

He wanted to become part of the solution, and thankfully, the skills he would need to help him succeed also ran in his blood. His uncle had been in the military but was killed in action in his prime. James's mom would say he was just like his uncle. True or not, James never got to meet him.

But if his uncle were here today, and he were anything like James, he would have to agree that Lily was not Michael Ronan's killer. Of that, he was sure. The hard part would be convincing Abrams.

Chapter Two

"Detective Rivers, I'm surprised to see you again."
Lily stood in the doorway of the funeral home, brushing
loose face powder from her black apron. "Excuse my
appearance. Mrs. Sherry needed a bit of touching up,
but she looks like her old self again. How can I help?"

As soon as James smiled at her, Lily knew she
would have trouble concentrating on the rest of her day.
The crinkles around his eyes made her heart flutter. The
softness of his face contrasted with the mouthwatering
muscular frame. The struggle to focus was real.

"Sorry to interrupt you while you're working, but I
wanted to ask you a few more questions."

Lily's stomach burned with nervous energy. "Is
there something wrong?"

"As you know, your sister Shanna provided us with
phone records and computer files of business
transactions. I spent the night looking through the file
but I wanted to clear up a few questions."

Lily's head started to pound. Even though she
knew she was innocent, he made her nervous. Maybe it
was the way he looked at her, or more like stared into
her. As if he were trying to envelop her with his eyes.
She would need to keep it professional, though. He
hadn't come to socialize.

"That's fine, but I need to finish Mrs. Sherry's
makeup. Can I work while you talk?"

He hesitated for a moment.

The true test of how he really felt about her job, she decided.

"Sure, that works for me."

Lily led him down the hall to her makeup room. Inside, a shiny white coffin had been placed in the center of the room. The lid was propped open, and within the coffin lay Mrs. Sherry's body. Her deep-berry dress had tiny navy-blue diamond shapes throughout the fabric. Apparently, the dress had been one of her favorites, and the family had also provided a golden silk scarf she wore almost every day. A light airbrushed wash of foundation brought her skin back to life, and a bit of taupe eye shadow gave her eyes dimension.

She put on her blue latex gloves to resume her work. "I hope this doesn't make you uncomfortable, but the family wanted the viewing done without embalming, which makes my job more time sensitive—if you know what I mean."

"I'm not uncomfortable. I see a lot of horrific things—not that what you're doing is horrific."

She chuckled at his anxious behavior. He seemed to be tiptoeing around what he had said before about her work. She liked that—not that it should matter to her. She wasn't interested in cops.

"I've never seen anyone put makeup on a body."

"Mrs. Sherry's family told me she wore a lot of blush, and my job is to have her look as she did when she was around them. I think that it's important to the family to have their last moments with their loved one feel like it did when she was alive."

James's eyes searched her face as if she'd said the

most fascinating thing he'd ever heard. She wasn't sure if she should go on or if she was totally freaking him out. She grabbed a large bore brush and began sweeping a rosy-colored shade of blush onto Mrs. Sherry's cheeks.

He watched her work quietly.

"There, that's much better," she said, standing back. "Don't you agree?"

James smiled. "She does look better. You're an artist."

Lily felt her stomach flip. No one had ever considered what she did on the same level as art. She certainly took pride in providing her best work, even if her clients couldn't talk back and give her feedback, but calling what she did art seemed like a stretch.

"I wanted to talk to you about Sarah Taylor."

Lily's mood fell. The name was familiar but not in a good way.

"She employed your services back in March for her mother's viewing. There were complaints made by her over the phone about the makeup not being to her satisfaction and other issues about the viewing reception."

"I vaguely remember this incident. Sometimes we get unsatisfied customers, just like any business does, but in her case, we did exactly what she wanted. The last thing I remember is she hung up on me and then called back to threaten our licenses. That was the last time I spoke to her."

"Based on the phone records, you don't get many complaints, but this one stood out."

"I don't think there's much to it. We just didn't see eye to eye. She should have been more clear about her

19

expectations if she was going to be so particular."

"Have you had any communication with her since the phone call?"

"No. Detective Rivers—"

"Call me James."

"James. I'm not seeing the connection here. I hope you didn't come all this way to talk about a customer complaint?"

"No, that isn't why I'm here."

She took a deep breath. "I'm sorry. I shouldn't have snapped. Sometimes I can't help myself." Lily was mad at herself for letting him see that side of her so soon. Fiery Mortician. That's what people in town had started calling her. She wished she could take her reaction back and make a better impression.

"No, you're right. I haven't told you the connection. I should've done that sooner. After reading the complaint from Sarah Taylor, I decided to call her."

Lily froze in place. She couldn't imagine what Sarah Taylor would have to say that would be at all relevant. Maybe she would rehash the whole incident and waste everyone's time?

"She told me all about the phone call you had with her back in March. All of that checked out."

Uh-huh. "As it should."

"But on a hunch, I asked her if she knew anyone by the name of Michael Ronan. She told me something very interesting."

Lily looked up from Mrs. Sherry.

"She told me Michael was her boyfriend, and he hadn't been home for two nights."

Lily's jaw dropped. Her mind spun in a thousand different directions.

Michael Ronan? Sarah Taylor's boyfriend? Dead in my basement?

"So, my question is, what was Sarah's boyfriend doing in your place of business?"

"Lily?"

A gentle knock came from behind the door. The door opened slowly. Shanna poked her head around the door. "Almost through? We've got a tight schedule today. Is that Detective Rivers?"

"It sure is. He came by for some follow-up questions," Lily replied nonchalantly, covering up the utter horror he'd just dropped on her.

"Is my sister in trouble, Detective? Should I call our lawyer?"

"No, she's not, but I'm not quite finished yet. After I speak with Lily, I'd like to set up some time with you, Zachary, and Antonio as well."

"I think maybe you can come up with another time to talk. I'm finished with Mr. Zhang's embalming, and he needs a little color to his face before his viewing." Shanna smiled. "I'd like to get him ready as soon as possible."

"Sure thing," Lily answered.

Shanna glanced at James one more time to show him she meant business and then shut the door.

"Understood. Can we meet at a more convenient time?" James asked. "Maybe after hours?"

Panic set in. Did he think she had something to do with the murder? "I tend to work very late. The cleanup process takes many—"

"This shouldn't take too long. We could go to Al's Diner if that feels less formal. Sometimes I stop in for the warm peach pie and scoop of vanilla ice cream after a long stressful day."

She scrunched up her face. "Really?"

"Yes, why?"

"Nothing. I would've thought a glass of scotch or whiskey was more your line."

He clamped down on his jaw, seemingly embarrassed by her comment. "I don't drink much—clouds the mind. I promise it won't take long."

Lily's shoulders relaxed a bit. Maybe this was more of a formality he had to follow through with. "If having a conversation with you helps end any suspicion you and Detective Abrams might have that Reynolds Funeral Home is somehow involved in Michael Ronan's murder, then I am happy to oblige."

And since she was mostly sure he didn't suspect her of any wrongdoing, she might actually enjoy a rare evening out—not in a romantic way, though, since she wasn't interested.

"Great. I'll let you get back to your work. I enjoyed learning about what you do. It was…fascinating."

"I'm sure it was."

"See you later tonight." He left the makeup room in a flash.

She hoped she hadn't made a mistake in agreeing to meet with him. Somehow the body of an unhappy client's boyfriend had ended up on her doorstep, and she would have to answer for it. At what point did she cease being the innocent bystander and instead become a suspect for murder?

Even if James was a breath of fresh air in this otherwise mundane town, she had to fight the urge to want to spend more of her time with him. She had to tread lightly and keep reminding herself that at the end of the day, James was a cop.

She didn't date cops.

****

Abrams stopped by James's office to check on the progress of the case. "Did you get a confession?"

"Of course not. She didn't do it."

Abrams smirked. "What did *you* get out of it? Flirting?"

James rolled his eyes. "Very funny. I told you I'm never dating again. Lily and I are meeting up at Al's, where we can talk more privately."

"Just the two of you? Sounds like a date."

"It's not a date. You know better than anyone. She does not fit the profile of a killer."

"She has easy access to body disposal—"

"The body was found on the floor in the basement," James retorted. "Not in one of their refrigerators or two feet from being incinerated."

"She likes dressing up the dead—"

"She's an artist. It's a form of art. Abrams, you collect weapons. Does that make you a murderer?"

Abrams narrowed his teeth and practically hissed a response. "Samurai swords. I have a collection of Samurai swords. Do you have any idea how expensive they are? You don't take those down from the wall to cut your steak."

"Innocent until proven guilty."

"Whatever you say. She's all we've got. I want that confession." Abrams walked out of the office.

"You're never getting one. She didn't do it." James responded even though the man had already left.

He stared down at Lily's handwritten notes. He couldn't deny how it looked. She had a motive. During their telephone call exchange, Sarah had threatened to report the business to the state, potentially annihilating a business that had been open for fifty years. That alone would make any business owner look for retaliation.

Then what? Lily plants Ronan at the funeral home to make it look like Sarah did it?

He couldn't believe it. He'd seen a lot of things, but this felt like a stretch. The idea of bringing her in as a suspect made him feel sick to his stomach. Abrams had to be wrong about this theory. He had a lot of experience, but he'd also gotten used to working in a sleepy town. Abrams wanted to close the case as fast as possible, but James wasn't convinced.

He glanced at his watch. Seven o'clock. Time to meet Lily.

Rising from his desk, he walked toward his car in the lot at the side of the building. The drive to the diner would be short, and he shouldn't have trouble finding parking after the evening rush hour. But his skin prickled, and his mind raced at the thought of meeting her alone. He never got nervous during an interview.

Was it her beauty swaying him toward her innocence? He hoped he had more integrity than that. Did he want to spend more time with her? Yes, her quirky occupation intrigued him, but Abrams was pressuring him to solve this case. Keeping Abrams happy was part of the gig. Not an easy task. Yet he couldn't deny the attraction he was beginning to feel for Lily might get him into trouble.

As soon as he saw her through the window, sitting at a booth, his heart thumped. The red flame of hair spilled down her back. Her cheekbones caught the light like a jewel. He reminded himself he'd done this a thousand times and knew how to be cool under pressure.

But one look at her smashed all of that to smithereens.

"You're late, Detective," Lily announced as soon as he walked into the diner.

She wasn't shy. He'd give her that. "Sorry, I've got a lot on my mind." He maneuvered himself into the booth opposite her.

"Am *I* on your mind?"

He froze, stunned by her abrupt manner. "You definitely are." She seemed a bit prickly today, no doubt defensive. His eyes flickered to the jukebox near the exit. Someone had chosen a slow song. The heat around his collar made him shift in his seat.

"It's not so crowded in here tonight." He looked around at the handful of people in various stages of their meals. "I take it you found an empty seat pretty quickly?"

"It wasn't so difficult."

The waitress approached their booth. "What can I get you two?"

"Apparently, there's a peach pie with vanilla ice cream I must try," Lily told her.

"Sure, I'll get that right away. Two spoons?"

"Why not?" James answered. "I might not be able to resist a bite. Unless you object?"

One of her brows rose. "Not at all. It was your idea, after all."

The waitress glanced back and forth between the two. "Great. I'll get that right out."

"Thanks."

In the bright fluorescent lights, James picked up on

a few things about Lily he hadn't noticed before. When she looked down at her hands, he saw the freckles dotting the center of her nose. The crown of her head had flecks of gold woven through it. She'd changed out of her black apron work attire and had put on a leather jacket over a black tank top. She looked like she'd purposely come with some armor to protect herself from him. He didn't like her feeling that she had to shield herself from him. He wanted her to feel safe with him, but her spunk did amuse him.

"Why are you smiling?" she asked.

"I don't know. You make me smile."

The waitress brought the pie and set it down in the center of the table between them, with two spoons. "Let me know if you need anything else."

"Thank you," James replied, adding, "The key is that it's warm, and with vanilla ice cream, you can't go wrong."

Lily picked up the spoon, slicing through the pie, and then scooped some of the ice cream and carried it to her mouth.

He watched her savor the dessert. Her greenish-gray eyes lit up the room. He could dive into them and imagine a happy existence, but at the same time, he knew that would be dangerous. His job kept him from giving anyone a normal life. Instead, he offered a steady stream of violence and bad guys.

"You were right. It's good. Now that I've had the pie, what did you want to ask me?"

Smart and beautiful. He hated that he'd come to interrogate her. His stomach ached with anxiety. "You said you didn't know Michael Ronan. Is that correct?"

"Never heard of him."

"But Sarah Taylor obviously knew him, and you knew her."

"I knew her as a client."

"An unhappy one."

He watched her take another bite of the pie. It made his mouth water.

"Tell me, Detective, have you looked into Ronan's personal life instead of focusing on who found his body?"

"I have. He had no prior record. He had a normal sales job. No kids. He liked to hang out in a biker bar called Metal Horse located in East Borough. I checked that out as well. It had a bunch of tough-looking guys but nothing illegal going on that I could tell."

"Biker bar? That didn't raise any red flags to you?"

"It's a free country. If you want to wear fangs and a cape at a dive bar for vampire night, that's your prerogative and is certainly not illegal."

"Maybe it should be."

"How conservative for a woman who shops for makeup to put on the dead. Speaking of which, we received the forensics report." He paused, wanting to evaluate her reaction. But her expression hadn't budged. "They identified a cosmetic powder on his shirt collar."

"And?"

"You gave me an in-depth tutorial of what you do for a living today, so I have no choice but to draw conclusions."

"He probably got that powder from hugging someone, or maybe he applied it to his own face."

Her answer wasn't good. It was great. She exuded the confidence in her answers that he needed to hear and bring back to Abrams. "Anything is possible, but nothing has been ruled out, including your interaction with Sarah."

She sat up straight. "Seriously, have you ever had an unsatisfied customer? Have you ever had a case go wrong?"

His mind flashed back to two years ago when the limp body of his girlfriend lay across his lap. There had been nothing he could do to save her in the crossfire. He had failed to protect her. After that day, he had vowed never to bring a civilian into his dangerous lifestyle again. He felt the sweat beads prickle his forehead and closed his eyes tight, fighting back the memory of that night.

"James?"

He opened his eyes and took a breath. "Sorry." Embarrassed by his vulnerable moment, he cleared his throat a couple times.

"What happened?"

"Nothing. You triggered a memory from my past."

She sat back and smiled. She seemed pleased that she had some effect on him. "Do you want to talk?"

"No. How about you answer my question now."

She leaned in toward him. "James, I don't know why Sarah's boyfriend was found dead at my funeral home. I've had no contact with her since that phone conversation months ago. She was pretty angry; maybe she did it."

"Why would she do that?"

"I don't know. That's your job." Lily shrugged her shoulders. "I guess she could have brought him to the funeral home to make it look like I did it."

"Is that your theory?"

"It just came to mind."

"Does Sarah hate you enough to kill her own boyfriend then try to pin it on you? Seems kind of extreme, doesn't it?"

"Like I said, that's your job. I don't know what's going on."

James knew this was no damsel in distress. Lily wouldn't make this easy on him, and it bothered him to question her like a suspect. It felt all wrong. His initial interviews with Antonio and Zachary had also yielded very little in the way of motives. He had so little to go on. "Zachary told me he didn't think he'd left the garage door open the day Michael had been killed. What do you think? Is Zachary the type to leave the garage open, inadvertently letting the killer in to dump the body?"

"Well, actually, yes, he is the type. He's a young man working in a funeral home. Guys his age are out partying in college. We've had a few incidents like that with him."

Everything she said contradicted Abrams's theory. He'll have to confront him. He took a breath and scooped up some of the pie with ice cream. Comforting himself seemed like the right thing to do at this moment.

"What's your theory?" she asked.

He hesitated. He could be straight with her or feed her a bunch of police mumbo jumbo. The choice seemed clear to him. "Honestly, I don't have one yet. I don't mind telling you that. I already told you, I haven't found anything on Ronan's side of the story. So far, he's as clean as a whistle. If the killer comes from your neck of the woods, who among you living in the

Reynolds house has triggered the need to murder? Does your brother have any enemies?"

"Not that I know of. He doesn't live with us, but he lives a pretty normal existence for a twenty-year-old. His girlfriend, Julie, is a good person as far as I can tell. She's studying to be a nurse."

"At his age, working in a funeral home is not normal."

Her eyes narrowed. "Here we go again with the judgments. It's not normal for *you*. I've been around the dead all my life. As a kid, I was obsessed with the makeup room. I wanted to be there all the time. The pots of jewel-colored powders. The brushes my mom used were similar to a painter's tools. There were even times when she had to make new facial features out of wax. I truly believed my mom had talent, and I became hooked."

He bit the insides of his cheeks, cringing at his own bluntness. Not his finest moment. He'd also never heard anyone talk about funeral homes in a positive and enlightening way. She intrigued him more and more each day. "It's amazing you can carry your mom's legacy forward. I didn't mean to be insensitive."

She looked away and smiled.

He saw from her expression she was proud of what she did, and he wanted to flatter her if it brought out that smile more often.

"What about you? What made you want to be a detective?"

"I think it largely runs in my blood. My uncle was also in law enforcement. My mom said we had a lot in common, but I never met him. He was killed in action."

"I'm so sorry. That's terrible."

Even when she frowned, she was beautiful.

"It's all right. It was a long time ago, and I don't remember it all that well."

Lily peeked at her watch. "It's getting late. Have I sufficiently answered all of your questions?"

"No, but I'm glad we had the pie."

"Thank you for the pie, Detective. If you think of anything else, you know where to find me." She got up from the booth. "I'm sorry about your uncle."

"Don't be. If it hadn't happened, I wouldn't have become a detective, and our paths would never have crossed."

"Are you talking about fate?"

"Only if you agree with me."

She smiled that kilowatt smile that killed him every time. "Good night, James."

She exited the diner, leaving him with more questions than answers. She'd stripped him naked in ways no one ever had. First, never would he admit he didn't have a theory already formulated on a case, and second, he never talked about his past with anyone. Lily Reynolds barely knew him, but already she had changed him.

Chapter Three

"This is the room where we have our viewings. There's plenty of space for up to sixty people, and we can provide refreshments for your guests to enjoy after the viewing," Lily said as she led a prospective client through a tour of the funeral home.

"Do you have options for music and floral arrangements? I'd like for people to feel at ease and comfortable. The last thing I want is for my guests to feel squeamish in a funeral home," Mrs. Jansen, the potential customer said.

Lily brought Mrs. Jansen back to her office. "We can play classical music of your choice, and you can have flowers delivered here the day of your viewing. I have a list of vendors who are all great choices."

"That sounds good." Mrs. Jansen took a seat opposite Lily and crossed her skinny trouser-clad legs. "But I have some concerns."

"Most do, but I'm sure we can find a solution."

"I'm not so sure."

Lily stopped riffling through the new registrant paperwork and stared at the client's glamorously made-up face. She looked to have some money; should she agree to hold the viewing here, that would be good for business.

"There's been some talk around town. People are saying there're bad things going on here."

Goosebumps rose on Lily's arms. She hoped the case of Michael Ronan hadn't leaked to the public. That would not be good. "Bad things?"

"My sister-in-law heard the cops found a dead body here with a pitchfork sticking out of his back."

"Pitchfork?" Lily immediately recognized the culprit—small-town gossip. But she didn't correct the mistake. She needed to deny everything.

"Yes, sounds so violent." Jansen put her hand to her chest. "Kathy, my sister-in-law, does not want her husband displayed in such a violent place, but I told her I would come and see for myself. I know Reynolds Funeral Home has a good reputation."

Lily had some damage control to do. "Mrs. Jansen, you know better than to believe the gossip. We've been in business for fifty years. You can't argue with that kind of experience and success."

The woman blinked false eyelashes that looked like spiders. "That's what I told Kathy, but news spreads fast in Manorview, and I only want the best service for my brother, Steve. May he rest in peace."

"And that's exactly what you'll get. Do you know what type of services you and your sister-in-law are looking for?"

"Why don't you tell me about them."

"We have full-service packages at different price points. The best-selling one is what we call the Five-Star Embalmer's Choice. It includes the full experience with client cleansing, followed by embalming with a top-of-the-line small-batch fluid selected specifically to fit the needs of each client. That is followed by expert makeup application to your specifications. Finally, you select the casket from our showroom and tell us what you'd like included at the reception in terms of food, flowers, and music. We can have live musical performances, buffet-style meals, and any type of flower arrangement you desire. There are other packages, but the Five-Star is the most popular."

Mrs. Jansen smiled. "That all sounds wonderful, but I need to speak to my sister-in-law first before committing to anything. If it were my decision, I would sign up right now, but she's in charge, not me."

"Maybe I can give her a call to discuss this further. Do you by any chance know who has been saying negative things about us to your sister?"

"We've been looking at funeral homes in the area, and Innovations Funeral Home was our other possible choice for Steve. The owner there—I think her name is Tina—she heard rumors about a violent death that happened here."

"It doesn't surprise me that a rival funeral home would say something negative about us. They probably want your business. Did Tina say who told her that?"

"Someone by the name of Sarah, I believe. Apparently, she knew the guy that died. But after talking to you, I'm not sure what's true or fiction."

Lily's mind went into overdrive. It didn't surprise her that her old rival Tina Collins would perpetuate nasty rumors—even though they were true—to steal clients from them. But to hear that Sarah was the one talking to Tina made Lily's blood boil.

She put on her signature saleswoman smile. "I can assure you, Mrs. Jansen—"

"Call me Veronica."

"Veronica. You're in the best hands here. We'll take very good care of Steve and your sister's needs."

"Thank you for taking the time to meet with me. I'll be in touch shortly about our decision."

"You're very welcome." Lily rose to walk her to the front door. "Please call us if you have any questions."

"I'll be in touch." Veronica walked out the door to her black chauffeured town car.

"Sounds good. Thanks for coming by."

Lily shut the door and let out a deep sigh. Sarah Taylor was single-handedly going to kill her family's business. To think an angry customer caused all of these issues. She wished to take it all back, the screaming on the phone, the hang-up. But at that moment, she truly believed they had provided the best service, as they always did, for Sarah's mother.

Lily walked toward the kitchen and lounge area of the house. Her stomach growled in a sign she desperately needed a break. The delicious scent of takeout permeated her nostrils. "What's for lunch?" she asked her brother and sister, who were already chowing down at the table.

"Chinese," Zachary garbled through a mouthful of fried rice.

"We got you shrimp stir-fry," Shanna said, scooping some out onto a plate for Lily. "How did your client meeting go? You look a bit disturbed."

"It didn't go that well. Mrs. Jansen came in to discuss a viewing for her brother-in-law, but it really felt like she was feeling us out." Lily popped a piece of shrimp in her mouth. The delicious nutty flavor of the sesame oil coated her tongue.

"Feeling us out?" Shanna asked.

"She heard about the murder." Lily lowered her

voice in between chews even though there was no one around to hear.

"Wasn't me." Zachary sniffed and took another huge mouthful of rice. His blue eyes gleamed innocently under his halo of reddish-gold hair.

"Did you tell your girlfriend?" Shanna quipped. "She's got a blabbermouth on her."

"No, she doesn't," he shot back, and a piece of rice flew out of his mouth.

"All right! Both of you stop," Lily snapped. "It wasn't either of them."

"Then who was it? Don Abrams wouldn't compromise his reputation by leaking any evidence," Shanna said. "Was it the new guy? Rivers? We know nothing about him. Maybe he leaked it?"

Lily's ears burned. The mention of James's name did things to her, things she'd been trying so hard to suppress. And failing miserably. "He didn't leak it."

"How do you know? You two have a flirty thing going on but—"

"He didn't leak it."

Silence.

She took a deep breath. *Caught.* Could she be more obvious? "I know who did. Someone named Sarah Taylor."

"Who's that?" Shanna asked.

"Remember the client who complained we didn't give her the services she wanted?"

"Oh yeah," Zachary said. "The screamer. Man, she was crazy."

"Yes, that one, and yes, she is beyond nuts."

"How did she hear about the murder?" Shanna asked.

"The dead guy was her boyfriend."

Zachary coughed, almost choking on his food.

"Oh, Lord." Shanna looked up toward the ceiling. "Who told you that?"

"James."

"*James.*" Shanna raised one eyebrow. "You two are on a first-name basis?"

Lily rolled her eyes and refused to answer that question. Shanna always knew when she was smitten with some guy. She had a history of catching on even before Lily knew how hard she'd fallen. *Infuriating.*

Two deep cleansing breaths later, Lily was able to continue. "When he didn't find anything on Michael Ronan's background, he contacted Sarah after reading those phone call notes I'd written about her complaint."

"See, Zachary, how important those phone notes are?" Shanna told him. "We would still have no idea who the dead guy is."

"Yeah, but until they find something better, they're looking at Lily for a motive," Zachary chimed in.

"Really?" Lily replied. "Do I look like a killer?"

"The cops are going to wonder how the dead guy ended up in our basement. Aren't they?" Shanna asked.

Lily shrugged. "I don't know. I guess."

"Does James think you had a part in it?"

"He didn't say that outright, but I'm sure he's thinking about it."

"It's completely absurd. All this from one angry phone call?" Shanna complained.

"I guess that's the best they've got."

"And now Sarah is talking about our business," her sister mourned. "She's going to ruin us."

"I got us all into this mess. I'm not going to let her

destroy what our family created fifty years ago."

"What will you do?"

Lily braced herself before dropping the bomb. They weren't going to like it. "I'm going to Sarah's house. I want to see if I can talk some sense into her before she turns the whole town against us."

Both her siblings looked at her like she'd lost her mind.

"Is that safe?" Shanna asked.

"Probably not. But I think it's worth trying to calm her down and talk to her."

"Do you want me to come with you?" Zachary asked. "As backup?"

"No. I'm trying to bring peace, not an entourage."

"I don't like it," Shanna said.

"We've got to do something. We're losing clients. A couple months of this, and the business will tank. We don't have a choice."

"What are you going to do about James? If he suspects you have something to do with the case, he's going to bring cops all over this place, and people will continue to spread gossip."

"If you handle Abrams, I'll handle James."

"You really think he's on your side?"

Lily's heart fluttered involuntarily. The feeling couldn't be wrong. "I know he is."

"Why?"

The truth. She had to tell the truth even though it would expose her feelings. "I can see it in his eyes."

****

I must be missing something, James thought as he drove slowly through the night toward Sarah Taylor's house in his beige undercover vehicle. If Lily had nothing to do with the murder of Michael Ronan, then James was definitely missing something on who was.

When he talked to Sarah on the phone to inform her of Michael's death, she had reacted appropriately. She'd cried and howled. She also had an alibi. She told him she was at home giving a client a haircut. She ran her own beauty business from her home. That client had corroborated her alibi.

Everything checked out, but yet he refused to believe that Lily had anything to do with it.

He'd already heard from Abrams about the negative press regarding the Reynolds place. Once he put two and two together, he realized the gossip had to be Sarah Taylor's doing. She wanted revenge.

That was when he decided to pay her a visit. Maybe shake her up a bit.

Sarah lived in East Borough, the rough part of town. He had some reservations about going in with no backup, but he knew Abrams didn't agree with his theory. He wanted to point the finger at Lily, yet James believed she hadn't done the crime. He felt it in his bones. In order to get his boss off his back, he needed proof.

Hopefully, tonight would be the night.

He turned onto Dune Street and let his car inch forward slowly toward her house. The houses were small, run-down. A few people sat outside on their front steps, soaking in the warmth. But as the sky dimmed, silence took over. An ominous feeling came over him, making him wonder if he'd made the right decision.

Too late.

He scanned both sides of the street thoroughly as he approached Sarah's house.

Number 303. Should be coming up on the left.

Out of the corner of his eye, he spotted a struggle taking place on the front lawn. The darkness enveloped the two figures, making it difficult for James to identify them. His eyes strained to see if either of them had a gun or knife.

Hard to tell. Proceed with caution.

He could easily get hurt if he intervened without thinking. The fight seemed unfair between such a mismatched pair. As the larger figure tried to pin down the other, the smaller one yelled out. James froze. The female voice rang in his ears. It couldn't be, could it?

Without thinking, he knocked the glove box open, pulled out his semi-automatic, and tucked it behind his back. The cautionary behavior he had been trained to use during this type of intervention flew out of his mind. A flash of red hair ahead propelled him out of the car and running toward the two figures.

As James prepared to slam his body against the larger figure, the smaller one smashed a rock into her attacker's head. The large one fell back just as James jumped on top of him. A right hook slammed into the man's cheekbone, causing James's knuckles to explode with pain. The two men grunted from exertion. One hard punch to the gut sent James off the perpetrator. He landed with an excruciating thud on his back.

Is that a rock digging into my flesh?

No, it was the gun he'd stuffed in his pants. He scrambled to his feet and pointed it at the man. The throbbing in his side and knuckles were dulled by adrenaline coursing through his body. Black-gloved hands went up in defense, but the ski mask made it impossible to see the attacker's face. Peering through the mask's slits were dark blue eyes and blood trickling down his left eyebrow.

James smirked. The blow to the head had been Lily. A mixture of pride and concern confounded his mind. He flashed his police badge with his other hand. "I saw the whole thing, buddy. Get down on your knees. Put your hands behind your back."

The perpetrator obeyed while James frisked him. A lump formed in his throat as he pulled a knife from the man's pant pocket. The idea that this guy almost used the knife to slice up Lily made his insides twist. James called for backup and finally took a moment to check on Lily. The gun stayed pointed at her attacker.

"Are you okay? Do you need an ambulance?"

She looked up at him with wide eyes.

He hated that look. It meant she was terrified, and he couldn't wipe tonight's events from her mind.

"No, I'm a little shaken up. But I'm fine."

"Help is on the way. We'll be out of here soon."

James turned his attention back to the assailant. "Who are you?" No response. He came in closer. Anger pulsed through his veins. Who did this guy think he was? Reaching out, he pulled the ski mask off in one quick tug. The other hand kept the gun pointed to his head. The man kept his eyes lowered to the ground. His disheveled brown hair had become matted with blood from the rock assault.

Convinced she would've handled the situation with or without him, James smiled on the inside. "What are you doing here?" He pointed toward Lily. "Do you know her?"

No answer. *Useless.* He'd dealt with this type of guy before. He wouldn't talk now, but he would in the interrogation room. James had a talent for getting confessions without using physical force. Four tense minutes went by, and a squad car finally arrived. James glanced at the arriving officers. He recognized Patrick Stern and Joe Richter stepping out of the vehicle and walking over to the scene.

"What do we have here?" Patrick asked in a deep baritone.

Every time James heard his voice, it made him think of a country singer, but the rest of him looked like a marathon runner—all lean and fit. His partner, Joe, played guitar in a metal band on the side. He kept his long, frizzy black hair tied back and hid most of his tattoos.

"He's not talking, but I witnessed him attacking her right out here. I subdued him before anyone got hurt. I figured we could take him in and see what we can get out of him later."

"Do they know each other?" Patrick asked.

"She says no. Not sure if this is random. But I think there's more to the story."

Patrick and Joe stood on each side of the man who still kneeled on the ground.

"Well, they always talk eventually. Once they hear the charges stacked against them and how much time they will do."

"Yeah, happens every time," Joe chimed in. "Especially since you witnessed the whole thing."

"All right, let's go, buddy."

The two cops reached down to lift the man up to his feet by his arms. They walked him to the squad car.

"Thanks for the backup," James told them.

"No problem. Kind of a slow night anyway,"

Patrick said. "Do you need an ambulance here?" He pointed to Lily.

"No, she hurt him more. She bopped him on the head with a rock."

Patrick smiled. "She should come work for us."

"Right," James replied, looking at the ground to hide his unease. Even though he had only engaged in mild flirting with Lily, the feeling was triggered from his past. That's all he needed, her caught in the line of fire again.

"See you back at the station."

"Thanks again."

As the squad car pulled away, James turned his attention toward Lily. She'd been crouched on the ground, ready to pounce if necessary. He reached his hand out to help her up.

"Are you sure you're not hurt?"

"Pretty sure. Maybe some bumps and bruises but nothing terrible. He's a big guy."

James clamped his jaw shut. He hated the sound of that. If he could have some time alone with that guy, he'd show him too. "Let's go," he told her. "I'll drive you home. We'll get your car in the morning."

Fighting the urge to take her hand, he followed her to his car. He opened the passenger door for her and took a moment to glance at Sarah Taylor's house. He wondered if she had anything to do with Lily's attacker. Problem was, he had no direct link between Sarah and the attacker. It would be a stretch to knock on her door now and question her. Plus, he didn't think Lily would be up for it after the ordeal she'd been through tonight. But he'd be back. There was no question about that.

Entering the car, he let the sanctuary of the quiet

enclosed space envelop them and provide a sense of calm before he opened up tonight's can of worms. "What happened?" he began.

She let out an audible sigh. "I came out here to talk to her. Bad idea."

"You mean Sarah?"

"Yes. She's been talking about the murder. It's spreading around town and hurting our business. Who wants to trust us with that stain on our reputation? I called her, and she agreed to talk. That should've made me suspicious, but I wanted to resolve it for us—for the funeral home. Little did I know she'd have that guy waiting for me. I should've known better."

"Yes, you should've. Never take a chance like that without calling me first. You could've been killed." His voice rose to unexpected levels at the risk of sounding tyrannical. Something about her alone out here at night with that guy waiting in the shadows to do what he wanted with her made his crazy, overprotective, and irrational side come out.

He shook his head to snap himself out of it. He couldn't allow those feelings to show. They had to be tucked down far within him, like all the other times he'd been around her and almost let something unprofessional slip.

It was best for both of them. At least that's what he'd told himself. "Sorry. I can't help myself. I'm trying to stay objective, but with you it's…not easy."

"It's okay. In fact, you're right. I shouldn't have come out here by myself. I should've at least thought of bringing Zachary with me. And I should really be thanking you."

Her innocent, wide-eyed expression gave him heart

palpitations. The protective instinct kept trying to claw its way to the surface, no matter how hard he tried to knock it down. In the past, things ended badly the last time he tried to protect someone, but the struggle to keep it all inside was almost more than he could bear. He put his hand under her chin. "You hardly needed any help."

She smiled. "What were you doing here? Did you follow me?"

The way her silver-green eyes stared up at him made him think maybe she hoped he had followed her. Technically, he hadn't, but he felt as if his subconscious had led him here to her. A long shot, but a feeling he still had, nonetheless. "No, you can feel safe knowing I am not stalking you. But I did have similar thoughts as you to come and talk to this Sarah Taylor person for more info."

"If you came to talk to her, does that mean you don't think I killed Michael Ronan?"

"I didn't say that but I can't rule out the possibility that she might be involved. I just need to find the connection between her and your attacker."

"Do you think he'll talk?"

"We have ways to get suspects to talk. Since he can't deny he attacked you, we can offer him a deal he won't be able to refuse in exchange for implicating Sarah. She probably hired him." Relief spread through him as the conversation turned back to the case. He had to keep his focus on the case and not on her lips. It was the only thing stopping him from trying to kiss her. For the sake of his job, for the sake of the case, and most importantly, for her sake.

He let out the breath he'd been holding in and

turned on the engine, grateful for the small amount of self-control that each day was dwindling by a thread. "That was a close one," he murmured under his breath.

"What was?"

Of course, she would hear him. She was sharper than the sharpest knife.

"Never mind. Let's get you home."

Chapter Four

Lily rocked her head from one shoulder to the other, trying to relieve the soreness in her neck. The scuffle outside Sarah's house the other night produced more than lasting psychological effects.

Frustrated, she tossed her makeup brush in a pile with the others and leaned back on the opposite counter. The dull ache in her neck made it difficult to lean over her clients. *How many pain relievers can a person take in one day?*

It was also a constant reminder of the incident, playing over and over in her mind. Thoughts of the poor decision she'd made to go over there, and what could've happened if James hadn't arrived when he did, plagued her mind. Vivid images of that night made sleep elusive. She'd already yawned seven times in the last hour.

Not to mention the near-constant thoughts of James. Though she tried, it was hard not to think about him. The protective way his eyes had flashed when he ripped off the man's ski mask. The way he hadn't hesitated even for a second to subdue her attacker. And how he'd looked at her like he was about to kiss her when they were sitting in his car. Her stomach fluttered. Still, she remained a suspect in his mind for the murder of Ronan.

Could that be holding him back from kissing her?

Or was it something else?

It dawned on her that none of this *should* matter since she didn't date cops. But she'd never felt this conflicted. Her priority had to be to clear her name and the business from any wrongdoing, or else her business would not survive.

After a deep, cleansing breath, she decided she would not continue to be the victim here. The idea that she was a suspect for murder made her skin crawl. Since no one else was willing to clear her, she would need to take matters into her own hands. She would have to solve the case of Michael Ronan. And she would have to suppress any feelings she'd developed for James. Her face scrunched at the thought of never getting to see him look at her in that puppy-love way. But the pressure to solve the case blinded him, and at this point, he would only get in the way.

Feeling more settled, she picked up the brush she'd put down earlier and worked to match the right foundation color to Ms. Oliveira's previously tan complexion. According to the family, she'd spent a lot of time in the sun in her travels around the world before her private jet crashed, and they wanted her to look as they remembered at her viewing later this evening. All she wanted to do was tune everything out and drown herself in work.

"Knock, knock." Shanna let herself into the makeup room. "How are you feeling?"

"A little sore, but better."

"Foolish—"

"Yes, I know, Shanna. I'm an idiot for going over there by myself."

"Why didn't you call James? You'd have had

yourself a willing bodyguard."

"And an accuser. He still thinks I may have been involved."

"That's not what you told us."

"Well, I'm not sure. It was a hunch. He hasn't said I'm innocent. Besides, you weren't this upset when I told you I was going to confront her."

"I should've been. It's my fault. I should've stepped in and told you not to go."

"You've been stepping in all my life. I appreciate that, but I made a decision on my own. Now I have to live with that."

"I trust you, but I don't know if I trust him."

Lily dropped her gaze, disgusted by her own conclusion. "Me either."

Shanna tapped the counter with her fingers. The air pressed down on them. "I've got an idea that will take your mind off your troubles."

"What's that?"

"The National Mortuary Conference is in the City today. We can leave now and drive there in time to check out some of the workshops. I know you've been wanting to get better at foundation matching, even though I think you're great at it—here's your chance."

Lily contemplated the idea. She needed a break from the funeral home. "Okay, I'll finish up with Ms. Oliveira, put her on ice, and then we'll be back in time for her viewing later tonight."

"Great. Should we take the hearse?"

"Why not? It's roomy and probably has more gas than my car does at the moment."

"Okay, meet you in the car. I'm driving since you're injured."

Normally, Lily would not agree to this arrangement. She hated when Shanna drove—so slow and cautious it gave her heartburn. But in this case, she would allow it. "Fine. Just this time."

They pulled out of the garage and onto the pebble-lined driveway. The pebbles allowed them to hear anyone who might be pulling up to their light-yellow Victorian-style house. Lily stared at the house as they drove away from it. She loved living there. The simple cozy style and quiet atmosphere made it homey and comforting. Shanna also lived in the house, but Zachary had chosen to live in an apartment in town, which was for the best—since he was the messiest person Lily knew.

An hour and a half later, Shanna pulled the hearse into the underground garage of New York's Convention Center. The enormity of the place always baffled Lily whenever she got to go to conferences or other meetings—a rare treat.

Once they reached the first floor, Lily's heart soared with excitement. She smiled at the huge banner that said, *Welcome, Morticians!* She loved her work and learning new techniques to make her even better at her job. This was a welcome distraction from all her problems.

They registered for the conference, and Lily scrutinized the list of workshops.

"Oh, I need to go to this workshop, *Smooth as Butter: Makeup Tricks for a Smoother Foundation Application*," Lily said, pointing to the brochure.

"That's a great idea. "I'm going to *Formaldehyde Free: Cleaner Methods for Embalming*. Seems like there's got to be healthier products to work with day in and day out than formaldehyde."

"You'd think. So we'll meet back here after our workshops."

"Sounds good."

Lily made her way through the crowd toward one of the many conference rooms on the floor. A mix of men and women poured into the workshop she had chosen. Golden cloth-covered seats lined up in rows to accommodate the large crowd. Lily found a seat toward the back and watched other morticians happily make their way in. A large projection screen filled up the wall ahead with the title of the workshop displayed on it in large letters. The presenter stood at the front, waiting for everyone to take their seat. Her blonde hair matched the seats.

As Lily sat there, she sensed the unmistakable feeling of someone staring at the back of her head. She turned toward the culprit. Tina Collins, the owner of Innovations Funeral Home, the only other funeral home in Manorview and, of course, her rival.

Tina quickly looked away when their eyes met. *An opportunity?* She couldn't let it slip by. This would be the perfect chance to see what Tina had to say to her face about the rumors she'd been helping to spread. After all, talking to Sarah was no longer an option. Lily loved her life too much to go down that road again.

Before she psyched herself out, she got up and approached Tina, sitting in the seat right next to her. Tina jumped when she noticed Lily.

"Did I scare you?"

She had that deer-caught-in-headlights look on her face but said, "No, I just wasn't expecting to see you here."

"Why? We have so much in common we're practically sisters. We both own funeral homes. I've seen you at Coffee Cup getting a late-afternoon black coffee like I sometimes do. Why wouldn't we sit together at a mortuary conference?"

"You surprised me, that's all." Tina clutched at her purse and shifted in her chair. True, it could be awkward to run into people randomly at events but not *this* awkward. *What was she hiding?*

"I think this workshop will be super-helpful. Don't you?" Lily glanced over at Tina, but her eyes stared up front where the speakers were getting the slide show ready for class.

"I suspect so."

"I heard you don't do the makeup yourself at Innovations. You have someone else doing it, right?"

Her eyes remained focused up front. "That's correct."

"Are your employees here with you?"

"No, they had client appointments today. I'll teach them if there's anything new to be learned from this workshop."

Lily rolled her eyes in frustration. *Doesn't she notice the elephant in the room?* Bad-mouthing her business, and all she got was small talk. Tina remained as frigid as an ice sculpture. This wasn't going to fly.

"Let's cut to the chase." Lily leaned in closer. "You already know why I came over. Why are you telling people lies about my business? You know that's hurtful to us, and it's not even true."

"What's not true? Everyone knows what happened. There's something funny going on over there."

Lily watched Tina's eyes dart back and forth, and

her fingertips dug into the leather of her purse. "You can't believe everything people tell you. Frankly, I'm a little disappointed in you. Trying to ruin another business is so petty. Don't you believe in karma?"

"No, I don't, actually." She relaxed the grip on her purse and then fluffed her short, curly brown hair. "I was simply stating the facts. People need to know what they're getting into when they go over to your place. It's only fair. I would want to know if I was spending my hard-earned money on a place with suspicious activity. You can't blame me for being honest."

Lily sat there, fascinated by her ability to twist the events. She also noticed Tina's hands trembled a bit as she put them out for emphasis. *Afraid? Of what?*

"I'd like you to stop talking about my business and spreading rumors. Manorville is big enough for both of us to make a living."

"I'll consider it." Tina finally looked straight at Lily. Her tiny, glossed lips quivered as she spoke. "I hear you know the detectives pretty well. It's no secret that Shanna and Abrams have dated in the past. Have they told you anything? Have they caught anyone yet?"

Taken aback by the question—and the quick change of topic—Lily hesitated. "Not that I know of, but why would the detectives tell me anything?"

"Why not? From what I've heard, you seem to have something going with James Rivers."

Lily's shoulders went back. "What is that supposed to mean?"

"I heard the young detective rescued you the other night like a damsel in distress. I bet he'd tell you straight away any news about the murder."

The only other person in the area that night was

Sarah. She had to be the one reporting back to Tina. That meant the two of them were in it together to bring down Lily and her business. Sarah, mad because her boyfriend was dead, decided Lily had something to do with it and started running her mouth. Tina would stop at nothing to crush her business. This was clearly a coordinated effort against Lily.

How they'd underestimated her. She wouldn't go down without a fight.

"Sarah doesn't know anything about me. She's a disgruntled customer whom you're exploiting for your own purposes. Not a very nice thing to do and for what? Is Innovations Funeral Home doing so poorly you need to resort to dirty tactics?"

Tina's face revealed nothing. Lily had not succeeded in getting a rise out of her.

"It seems I'm too late. You've already been brainwashed by speculation and rumors. I've known you for a long time, and I really thought you were smarter than that, but you can't reason with pure evil."

"You don't know who you're dealing with," Tina said, standing. "I've heard enough from your mouth. You watch yourself." Her pointer finger jutted out. "This is just the beginning."

Clearly flustered, she dropped her purse. In one motion, she snatched it up, but in doing so, something dropped out. She quickly turned to leave, not noticing her mistake, and walked away, leaving the item behind.

Lily picked it up. *A photo.* Her stomach flipped as she gripped the image tighter. Her mouth dried up like sandpaper. She couldn't believe her eyes.

The photo was of Michael Ronan and Sarah Taylor smiling in each other's arms—a strange thing to have in light of the recent circumstances. An innocent person wouldn't carry around a photo tying them to the victim unless they were involved in some way. But what had been Tina's role?

Lily stuck the photo in her back pocket and failed miserably to pay attention to the rest of the workshop. She had a bomb in her jeans, and she didn't know how to proceed. Her instincts told her to hide it until the right time came up, but that seemed cowardly given all the trouble that Tina had caused lately.

She sucked in some calming air. *Breathe.* She shook her head. *No.* She would not act on strong emotions. She would hold on until the right moment showed itself, and when it did…Tina Collins better look out.

****

"Who's the perp?" Abrams asked without even saying good morning as he entered James's office.

"Tom Bleyer. He's not saying much, though."

"Can he be linked to Sarah Taylor?"

"We went through his phone records, computer hard drive, and bank statements. I didn't find any link to her. Besides, where would she get the money? Hitmen don't come cheap."

"She had enough money to pay for funeral services. Why wouldn't she have enough to pay for a hitman?"

"She performs beauty services from her home and lives in the East Borough neighborhood. She wasn't exactly rolling in money, but I found a copy of her mother's will. She left her some money for the funeral services. Might there be some money left over?"

"Maybe. What was Lily doing there that night?"

"She said she wanted to go over there to talk. Sarah's been spreading rumors about the murder around town. It's affecting their business."

"And what were you doing there?"

James bit the insides of his cheeks. He knew where Abrams was going with his line of questioning. It didn't do great things for his credibility. "I went to see if I could get something out of Sarah that might help the case. Turned out to be the right decision to show up when I did. Now we have the perp, and Lily's safe."

Abrams tightened his lips into a hard line. "Yes, lucky for her you were there, but I hope you aren't purposely throwing this case off. For the murder of Michael Ronan, your target is Lily Reynolds, not Sarah Taylor."

Rivers threw his hands up. "I have no proof." He rubbed his face in frustration.

"Then what's your theory?"

"I don't have one yet, but the evidence is pointing to Sarah, who is clearly trying to kill Lily. She should be the one in here."

Abrams shuffled his feet and rubbed his whiskers. "All right, I'll humor you. Let's go with that theory. Why would Sarah want to kill Lily? Because she thinks Lily killed her man? That's more of a reason to focus on Lily. Stop being a hero and get the perp to confess. If he admits Sarah placed a hit on Lily, then you can bring her in for questioning. Maybe she's got more to say about the case."

"I know that."

"Then get back to it." Abrams slapped the desk with his hand and walked out of the office.

But James couldn't get back to it. Consumed with

thoughts of Lily all morning, he'd been too distracted to focus on getting a confession. Images of her full lips and how close he'd come to kissing her taunted him. That night in his car, he'd done everything he could to hold back, but how much longer would that last? And yet his past loomed over him like a phantom, pulling him back from what he wanted. As much as he wanted to, he couldn't ignore it. Not for Lily's long golden-red hair or her shimmering silver-green eyes. Not even for her irresistible fiery nature.

Exhausted by the conflict in his mind, James put his head on his desk. Who was he kidding? All he did was think about her. How was he supposed to function like this? And with Abrams breathing down his neck to solve this case, he might just go nuts. He had to do something to get his mind off her.

Before another minute went by, James lifted his head from the desk and walked out of his office. He sped down the long corridor toward the holding cells. The station had three cells capable of detaining approximately thirty prisoners—not that Manorview ever saw much crime. Most of the time, the cells were empty and Jimmy, the guard in charge of it all, spent his shift watching videos on his phone. James approached the guard desk on a mission.

"Hey, Jimmy, bring out number two. I want to talk to him again."

"Again? He ain't gonna talk. I'm trying to finish this episode of my show."

"Just bring him, please."

"Damn it." Jimmy paused his show and went to unlock the keys from the cabinet.

James stood in the interrogation room waiting as

Jimmy brought back Lily's attacker and handcuffed him to the chair.

"What's the matter, James? You got nothing else to do today?" Jimmy scratched the graying curls at his temple. "Man, you're wasting your time with this guy. He ain't gonna talk."

"All right, all right. Don't worry, it'll be different this time. I have a plan—a better one. Thanks, Jimmy."

"No worries. Take your time. I've got three episodes left in this show I've been watching called *Simply Me*. It's about a single mother who has to start over again in a new town and how she has to reinvent herself to get by as the sole provider for her kids." Jimmy's voice cracked before he finished his sentence. He cleared his throat. "Sorry, didn't mean to lose it there. It's a sad story."

"No worries. You go enjoy it. I'll let you know when I'm done."

"You got it." Jimmy put the key ring in his pocket and left them alone.

James stared at the man seated in front of him. Tom was a large man. A very large man. Images of what could have been Lily's fate crawled back into his skull. James shook it off. He needed to stop thinking about Lily if he was ever going to accomplish anything.

Tom's eyes were downcast. The dried blood remained matted in his hair.

James pulled out his mini cassette recorder from his pocket and placed it on the table in between them. "Let me break it down for you real simple, Tom. If you don't talk, we have no choice but to send you away for a very long time. If you talk, we can work on lessening the charges. So, what'll it be?"

Nothing.

James pulled the chair out and sat opposite Tom, forcing him to look at his face. "Look, man, I don't know why you're being so loyal. Did Sarah hire you? She doesn't care what happens to you. She can't get you out of this mess." James leaned in closer to Tom. "She's out there in the world, free as a bird, and you're here, chained up to that chair. Why are you protecting her?"

Nothing.

James stood up and turned toward the wall, rubbing his chin. He didn't care anymore what it took. He would get a lot of heat for what he was about to do, but he didn't care. He needed answers. Turning back around, he dropped the bomb. "We'll drop all charges."

Within seconds, Tom looked up. Bloodshot eyes. Blank expression. But at least he was listening.

James placed both of his hands on the table in between them and stared down at Tom. "Who hired you?"

"You already know. Don't need me to tell you."

"Yes, I do. The legal system doesn't run on guesses."

Tom swallowed a few times. "I need some water."

James straightened his back and breathed in a frustrated breath. "Sure. I'll get you some water." He knocked on the door. "Jimmy, let me out. Perp wants some water."

"Oh, that's a step up from catatonic." Jimmy grabbed the keys out of his pocket and unlocked the door. "You've made progress. I spoke too soon."

"Wouldn't you buck up if I gave you a get-out-of-jail card?" James asked, walking over to the water cooler and grabbing a paper cup out of the dispenser.

"Wouldn't we all?"

James didn't answer as he poured the water and walked back into the room. "Leave it open. He's not going to run now."

"Sure thing, boss."

James handed Tom the cup.

He drank it greedily.

That didn't surprise James. Tom had been sitting in a holding cell for days, refusing to eat or drink anything. Now that he'd be getting the golden ticket, it made sense he'd turn back into a human.

"Who hired you?"

Tom pursed his lips before he decided to talk. "Sarah Taylor."

Finally. He got him. "Why did she hire you?"

Tom looked down again. "Man, I told you what you wanted to know. Now let me go."

"Look, I gave you a present. The least you can do is answer my questions. Did she tell you why?"

"Why what?" Tom refused to look at James.

"Why she wanted to get rid of Lily?"

"Sounded like small-town nonsense."

"I'll be the judge of that."

"She said she was told by her friend—I think her name was Tina—that someone by the name of Lily killed her boyfriend. That's why she hired me—for revenge. I don't ask a lot of questions. I just do the job. People have all kinds of reasons to kill one another."

"I know that."

Tom stared up at James. His eyes narrowed. "Sarah wanted Lily to suffer as retribution for her boyfriend. She told me I could do whatever I wanted as long as

Lily sensed the terror of knowing she was about to die."

No words. James had no words. *The horror. The anger.* His blood boiled. But he didn't react. His training kept him level-headed in the interrogation room. A perp would try to shake you up, but you didn't take the bait. James's body didn't want to listen. His fingers ached as he pumped them into fists. Heat emanated from his body. He wanted to lean across the table, pop him in the face until you couldn't tell who was bleeding more. The image of Tom's blown-up face made James smile.

"What's so funny?" Tom asked.

"One of these days, you'll end up back here in this same seat, and when you do, there will be no deal. I look forward to that day. Until then, you better tell me everything you know."

"Man, I told you everything."

"Did Sarah say anything else about Tina? Does she live nearby? Does she have a family? Anything?"

"Not really. She said Tina worked with dead people. I don't know what that means. I thought she was joking. Who works with dead people?" Tom scrunched up his face. "After I'm done with them, I don't care what happens to them. Not my problem."

"It's someone's problem though, right?"

Tom shrugged his shoulders. "I told you everything I know. We had a deal." His voice rose in anger.

"All right, you cooperated. I'll have Jimmy get the paperwork together, and then you can go. You got off this time, but you are definitely on our radar. My advice to you—find a better job." As James left the interrogation room, he walked past the guard desk and spied Jimmy staring at his phone. "All set, Jimmy. I'll get started on the documents to let him out."

Jimmy's eyes never left the screen. "Sounds good, boss. Whatever you say."

James walked back to his office, drained. He sank into his chair. Getting Tom to confess had exhausted him. It was the least favorite part of his job, along with the paperwork. He liked being outside in the action, catching killers and taking them off the streets. That part felt satisfying.

As far as Tina went, if she worked with the dead, she was either a coroner or a mortician like Lily. If that was true, then Lily and Tina must know each other. He couldn't tell yet where the bad blood was coming from, and Lily hadn't mentioned anything either. Sounded like Tina was the instigator in this case, and Lily was the victim.

So who was Tina?

Chapter Five

After the last client left for the day, Tina Collins sat at her desk, staring at the schedule, and sighed at the short list. Not good.

Business was not doing well. And why?

She didn't understand it. She'd opened its doors five years ago with a little inheritance and a dream. She thought she was a savvy businesswoman with the creativity and staff to get things off the ground, but lately, the number of clients was dwindling. And yet Reynolds Funeral Home continued to bring in client after client. Tina slammed her fist against the desk. How did they do it?

Chris, her well-trusted manager, poked his head in the door. "Everything all right here?"

She gestured for him to come in and sit in one of the beige suede-covered seats. "Sort of."

He stepped in and shut the door. "What's wrong?"

"A lot. I just don't get it. How do they do it?"

Chris sat and crossed his dark gray trouser-clad legs. "How does who do what?"

"Reynolds Funeral Home." She stabbed her pen into the schedule for emphasis. "How do they keep attracting customers while our numbers sink to the ground?"

He stared at the upright pen. "They've got the history behind them. People like knowing they've been in business for so long."

"It's got to be more than that. How is our staff performing? Any complaints?"

"Marcia is always meticulous with makeup application, and Simon is more than qualified to embalm. He knows all the latest techniques. I don't see any issues with staff."

"Good. I always wondered why Lily and Shanna insist on doing all the work themselves and if that made a difference in getting more business."

"No, they're both great. I think with the scandal that's going on over there we'll see more business come our way."

Tina's eyes narrowed. "Terrible tragedy, that Ronan case, but I suspect it should draw more clients."

"Hopefully. And there's no chance that you and Lily can reconcile and join forces? You could have one large funeral home empire together. Think of the possibilities. With your talent for innovation and her client list, you two would rule the funeral services market."

Her skin prickled with heat. The temperature in the room had risen a few degrees. This was a sensitive topic. "Not a chance. There are some things that can never be forgiven."

"If it was so long ago, maybe it could be just water under the bridge?"

Although innocent, his comments did nothing but bring back painful memories. The kind no child wanted to remember. Tina's dad had been involved with insider trading crimes for years. He finally got caught on the fifteenth of May—a date she'd never forget on the front page of the local newspaper. After he was convicted,

Rick Johnson was hit with a sentence of thirty years in the state pen.

The cop who caught him? Bruce Reynolds, Lily's father.

Tina was just a kid when her dad was sent away, and she'd been devastated. Years went by, He wasn't there to see her win the Junior Entrepreneur contest in middle school. Back then, she'd created a business selling an all-natural, dissolvable capsule that neutralized harmful prescription drugs that people threw out into the trash and eventually harming the environment. It had its own issues, such as the cost to produce the capsule—astronomical and cost-prohibitive for any real-life application—but the process had gotten her interested in science, and that led her to mortuary school. She was particularly proud of her achievement.

As time went by, Tina and her mom regularly visited her dad in prison, which to Tina remained equally as devastating as when he was first sent away. But then the worst thing of all happened. On a day in early October, he escaped from prison and sought revenge on Bruce Reynolds. He went to their house that night and shot Lily's parents. Shortly thereafter, he turned the gun on himself.

All these years, Lily and her siblings remained completely oblivious. They knew an escaped prisoner had killed their parents out of revenge, but they didn't know Tina's dad was the escaped prisoner. And because she now had a different last name—due to a previous marriage—the Reynolds family never put two and two together.

Tina held back the tears threatening to spill down her cheeks. Lord knows she'd cried enough over the years. But not today. She couldn't let Chris see her at her weakest. That wouldn't be good for morale.

"It will never be water under the bridge," she said sadly. "There's too much bad blood."

Pressing his lips together, he frowned. "In that case, we need to come up with a new strategy to attract customers. Should I call the staff in for a meeting?"

"Good idea. We do need a plan."

As she watched him leave her office to go out and raise the troops, it reminded her of why she'd hired Chris in the first place. Although his résumé was relatively short, due mostly to his youth, he had been a manager in a retail shop in town—that meant a lot. He easily adapted to the needs of the business above everything else and had become one of the best managers she'd ever hired—and there'd been quite a few before him. She valued him as her employee.

Less than two minutes went by before he returned, with Marcia Alonso and Simon Cook following close behind. The three of them sat on the couch opposite Tina's desk. Marcia had on her denim jacket, and Simon had on his hoodie. Both looked ready to leave for the day.

Marcia's eyes were wide, like a hunted gazelle's. That didn't surprise Tina. She was easily intimidated. Simon, on the other hand, sat on the edge of his seat, looking like he was up to execute whatever task was needed.

"I know it's close to quitting time, but Chris called you both up here for an important reason. As you know, the schedule has been kind of light the last several months. We can't survive much longer; equipment and supplies cost money. The house isn't going to pay for itself, and your salaries need to come from somewhere."

A small gasp left Marcia's mouth as she reached over to the end table and pulled some tissue out of the box. Simon rested a hand on her shoulder in a gesture of comfort.

"I didn't call you two up here to fire you," Tina stated as clearly as she could. "Let me just get that out of the way. Don't worry, I certainly have had ups and downs in my life, but I am no quitter."

Marcia let out her breath. "That's a relief. I just signed a lease on a new apartment in this neighborhood, and there's no way I can afford it without this job."

"I'm not closing our doors yet, but we're going to need to make some changes to attract more customers. I've been doing a lot of thinking about each of your skills. Marcia, I know you are a talented artist. You showed me your portfolio when you interviewed here, and makeup is an artistic expression, but I know you are capable of much more. Here's what I'm thinking."

Tina pulled out a folder and handed it to Marcia. "I'm no artist, but I drew up some sketches of what I call coffin art. We're going to be offering clients the choice of getting designs right on the outside of their coffins."

"I like this one." Marcia held out a drawing of a white coffin with an American flag etched into it.

"I think people will really like that one, too. There are endless possibilities for what people want on their coffins. Maybe someone wants a religious symbol on it or a favorite hobby. I know you have the creativity to help people realize those desires. What are you thinking?"

Marcia flashed a set of dimples and bright white teeth. "I think it's a great idea, and I love being able to branch out into other forms of art."

"Simon, I went to the mortuary conference in the City the other day." Tina sniffed as she worked to suppress thoughts of her confrontation with Lily there. Her threats may have thrown Tina off her game—sort of. "I brought back some new equipment to speed up the embalming process. We can cut the time in half and take on more clients per day. Clients will be able to hold their viewing sooner than before, and that will allow them to resume their normal lives at a faster rate. I also want to look into different embalming fluids that offer various scents and colors to the skin. I want to make Innovations Funeral Home exactly what I've named it—modern and innovative."

"Sounds good to me. I've been reading up on the latest techniques," Simon added. "There are definitely new approaches out there to implement."

"Great. I don't want you two to worry about your jobs. Together, we'll get this place recognized and as well known to everyone as the Reynolds place."

"Speaking of the Reynolds," Chris said. "Simon, have you been in contact with Zachary recently?"

"He was at Jake's Beer Hall a few weekends ago."

"Did you talk to him?"

"I did. I asked him how he was holding up."

"He said things were a little stressful lately with all the drama going on about the murder case. He said everyone is preoccupied with trying to cooperate with the cops and helping to find the killer."

"Do they have any suspects?" Tina asked.

"Zach didn't say. He talked a little bit about the

day the body was found. He wasn't the one who found it, though. It was Lily."

"How convenient," Tina added.

Simon shifted in his seat. "Oh, and he did mention something I thought was interesting."

"What's that?" Tina leaned in closer.

"He said he thought maybe Lily was in love with one of the detectives."

Tina's face fell. "How disappointing. That'll take the focus off her."

"You really think she did it?" Simon asked, rubbing one side of his crew cut.

"Of course she did it. She has the motive. All the Reynolds family cares about is keeping their business alive at anyone's expense. If Lily felt Sarah Taylor was threatening the future of the mortuary, she would stop at nothing to save it."

"Hey, I'm with you one hundred percent," Simon swore fervently. "I'll do whatever it takes for Innovations to get ahead."

"That's the spirit." Tina smiled. She knew there was a reason she had hired him. During his interview, she'd felt his passion for embalming, but also his loyalty had shone through.

"Good meeting, guys. Thanks for everyone's hard work. We'll see you in the morning." Chris said, wrapping up the meeting. He stood up to walk the two out.

Marcia and Simon left without another word. Chris followed them to close the office door, and then he walked back over to the opposite wall and leaned against the windowpane while staring out into the almost empty parking lot behind the funeral home.

"This whole thing about Lily and the detective, James somebody or other, is probably bar talk," Chris said. "It'd look really bad for Don Abrams if his new recruit was caught screwing around with a suspect."

"Yes, it would," Tina agreed, "but Abrams also has a taste for the Reynolds family. He's been hooking up with Shanna for years now. She might be the older and wiser one of the sisters, but her taste in men defines incompetence at its best."

Chris turned away from the view and looked at Tina. "Anyway, I wouldn't worry too much about Reynolds Funeral Home."

"Why's that?" Tina asked, wary of the confidence in Chris's tone.

"The damage is already done."

Chapter Six

Lily watched patiently as Tina's car pulled out of the parking lot of Innovations Funeral Home and drove away. She'd hidden behind the thick trunk of a nearby oak tree while waiting for each of Tina's employees to leave the facility so she'd have a chance to break in.

Breaking in.

Had she completely lost her mind? Maybe. But once she'd seen the photo Tina had of Sarah and Michael, her ears had pricked up like a hound dog during hunting season. What was a business rival doing walking around with that photo? In addition, her nervous, twitchy behavior at the mortuary conference made it look like she knew something. Lily wanted to find out what.

She thought about going to James with all this, but he had Abrams in his ear, still trying to convince him she was the main suspect. Why would he listen to her with that kind of pressure from his superior? Added to that, she couldn't think straight around him. Those sky-blue eyes hypnotized her every time. Not to mention the trouble of her self-imposed rule of never dating cops. Nope. She had to solve this one herself.

That's how she found herself creeping up to the back door of Innovations with the hope of finding something to incriminate Tina and would remove herself from the list of suspects. She'd never broken into anything in her life, but a quick search online led her to obtaining a crowbar, then an expired credit card to use for sliding open the latch. She had no idea if either tool would work, but at this point, she'd try anything to get the heat of the investigation off her back.

The crowbar didn't slide in as easily as she'd hoped. In fact, it barely went in at all. Drat! She hadn't thought to bring a hammer. Lily racked her brain.

Come on, Lily, you're resourceful—think!

She looked around until her eyes landed on the target. A rock. That should do it. She reached down and picked it up. The flatter end would work perfectly against the metal bar. She hammered the crowbar into the opening of the door with all her might. It wasn't fast, nor was it quiet. The loud smack of the rock against metal made this way too noisy for a covert operation, but this way she'd get in faster. No one should be inside anyway.

Pounding away at the crowbar, Lily felt the door open easily—too easily. She took an awkward step forward, almost falling as the door pulled away from her. Standing in front of her with a look of surprise on his face was the manager of Innovations Funeral Home, Chris Tuchman. Lily's stomach plunged to her knees.

"Lily? Is that you?"

"Chris? I didn't know you'd still be here."

"What are you doing?" He looked at her crowbar. "Are you trying to break in?"

She took a deep breath. She had no other explanations he would believe. The truth always comes out. "Frankly, I'm not going to tell you what I'm doing. Since you're the manager here, I know you're aware of what's going on between Tina and me. If you know what's good for you, you'll stay out of our business."

His lips twitched. "You can explain to the cops what you were doing. They should be here any minute."

"Cops? I'm not a burglar, Chris. I told you this does not concern you."

"So instead of calling on the phone or knocking on the door, you used a crowbar to get in?"

Stunned into silence, she could make a break for it and run. He wouldn't chase her. Or she could wait and give the cops her elaborate story. Chris wouldn't really press charges, would he?

The headlights of the car pulling up created a spotlight on the two of them. Blinded by the light, she couldn't see who had stopped in front of them. A figure came out of the car and walked slowly toward them. Lily crossed her arms in defiance. Let them try and take her down. The fire deep in her belly would come out if need be.

The figure walked in front of the headlight, effectively blocking it. Now she knew who had responded to Chris's phone call. Her heart pounded in reaction to seeing James walk toward them but not with fear—with exhilaration.

"Is this your frightening intruder? Should I bring shackles for both her arms and legs?" His haughty smile infuriated her.

Chris frowned at James Rivers's dismissive comment. "I'm the manager here. I was finishing up some work in my office when I heard a loud pounding noise. Sounded like someone was trying to break in, which is why I called 9-1-1. I came down to find Lily Reynolds trying to break into our business."

James glanced at Lily. She felt the weight of judgment from his stare. "Who owns this business?"

"Tina Collins," Chris replied smartly. "This is a funeral home."

Lily noticed a change in James's posture. The crinkles around his eyes that she loved so much relaxed.

"Thank you," James said. "I'll take it from here."

She knew by the artificial tone in his voice that he was trying, but failing, to be serious. He turned toward Lily with a straight face. "Ma'am, I'm taking you in for questioning." Then he led her to the passenger side of the car and opened the door.

Lily glanced at Chris. He had a smug look on his face. Little did he know she wanted to go with James. Her heart and mind were in constant battle whenever she laid eyes on him. She'd left her house hell-bent on steering clear of him today and working on the case on her own, but even a brief look at the snake tattoos coiling around his biceps made her weak. She would go with him this time. She had no choice.

Lily stepped into his car. She watched him walk around to his side. He got in, shut his door, and started to turn on the ignition. She looked for Chris, but he'd disappeared. He'd retreated and closed the back door.

"I turn around for one second, and you're off committing more crimes. How am I supposed to believe anything you say?"

Even though he was teasing her, the anger bubbled to the surface. "I don't commit crimes." She sucked in an exasperated breath while shaking her head.

"Why are you so annoyed? Breaking and entering is a crime."

"I realize that, but at this point, I'm desperate."

James pulled out and drove slowly through the streets. She knew he wasn't taking her back to the station. He'd probably convinced a cop to let him handle the call once he'd heard it was at a funeral home. It wasn't a long drive back to the funeral home, but he seemed to want to take his time.

Yet he remained quiet—too quiet, which made her realize she might have hurt his feelings. She'd gone too far, as usual. She wished she could take back what she had said, but the truth was it was only a matter of time before she fired away at him again.

"I know why you came here," he said, breaking the awkward silence.

"You do?"

"Tina Collins. You think she had something to do with the murder."

"Have you been following me again?" Lily watched him smirk at her comment.

"No. I finally got the guy who attacked you to talk. Tom Bleyer, hired hitman extraordinaire. A real winner with great values. He said Sarah hired him."

"Obviously." Her impossible-to-control mouth went off. Again.

James didn't take his eyes off the road. "He was given some pretty unsettling instructions from Sarah on how to *deal* with you."

Lily swallowed. She'd had plenty of sleepless nights since the attack but would never admit to it. A strong portrayal of strength was paramount to her survival. That was something she learned at a young age after both her parents were savagely killed.

It was the universe telling her, *buck up, kid, you're on your own.*

"How was this Tom supposed to deal with me?"

"It doesn't matter now. I wanted to pound his head into the ground. People like him have no purpose on this Earth. But I had no choice. I had to cut him a deal to get the information."

"What else did he tell you?"

"He said Tina was the one who told our friend Sarah you were the killer. I'm guessing that's why I'm finding you trying to break into her business?" James pulled up to the Reynolds Funeral Home and turned off the ignition. "Why does everyone think you killed Michael Ronan?"

Her eyes welled up with tears. She was tired of fighting the cops, the town gossip, and anyone else who wanted to start trouble. She was tired of being strong. She was tired of it all. "I'm an easy target. But I'm not going to defend myself to you. If you think I did it, then get it over with and arrest me."

"I'm not going to arrest you." He looked at her with soft, glowing eyes that seemed resigned to whatever came next. "But I am going to kiss you."

Lily's stomach clenched. She wanted to let go and not question every decision she made. But who was she kidding? Then she'd be a different person. "Why would you do that? I'm a criminal, aren't I?"

"In my heart, I never believed you had anything to do with the Ronan case. I think you know that, and I think…you want to kiss me too."

If her stomach clenched any harder, it might disappear. But he was right. She did want to kiss him.

James leaned toward her. He lifted her chin up to meet his lips. She'd expected them to be soft, and they were. They were also noticeably full and a part of him she'd thought about quite frequently. But she couldn't have known how he'd use them. Soft and cautious at first but quickly deepening into a sultry experience that awakened her body and made her want more.

As the heat between them rose a notch, he pulled himself away from her, frowning as he looked away.

"What's wrong?"

He leaned his forehead against the steering wheel, clearly struggling. "We shouldn't...I can't."

It hurt—but he was right. Again. "Same here. I agree. We can't."

He lifted his head away from the steering wheel. "You do?"

"I don't date cops."

"Because of the danger involved?"

Lily took a deep breath. She didn't want to talk about her past, but she owed him an explanation for her own reluctance. "My dad was a cop. He and my mom were both murdered by an escaped prisoner whom he helped put away. I guess you could say I'm not interested in going through that again. Like you said, it's a dangerous job, and I don't know if I can handle another hit."

He sighed. "I'm sorry you went through that. It is part of the job and accepting that is hard for most people. I respect that, and...I can relate. Two years ago, my girlfriend died in my arms after she was caught in the crossfire of a gun battle. I couldn't save her. After that day, I vowed never to allow anyone to get too close to me again, knowing that could happen again. It's just too risky."

"Wow. That's horrible."

Lily stared out the window. It all made sense now.

His reluctant behavior toward her. The way he seemed to be holding back on every level. Selfishly, she felt relieved it hadn't been about her. It wasn't about the case or her. It was about his demons. Similar to hers. They had more in common than she could ever imagine. And yet knowing the truth didn't really change anything for them.

"I'm sorry, too. No one should have to see someone they love die that way." Reluctantly, she opened the passenger door. They were at an impasse that could not be resolved tonight. But even so, she held onto the small shred of hope that they could let go of their pasts someday. "I guess we're both scarred." She got out of the car and leaned in through the window. "Thanks for covering for me tonight." Although, if she had to be arrested, part of her wouldn't have minded if it was ordered by him.

"Not a problem. Abrams and I can bring your car over tomorrow. And Lily, one more thing." He leaned in closer to her. "None of this is your fault—the murder, the scandal, even what happened to your dad. But please don't try to solve the case on your own. It's too dangerous. I couldn't live with myself if something happened to you."

At first, her heart throbbed from the impact of his sentimental words. For the first time, she believed him. She'd spent so much energy wondering how he felt about her and if he thought her innocent. She should've felt settled. She should've felt vindicated, and most importantly, she should've been swooning.

But her tough side pushed its way through, making sure she didn't cave. She returned a wicked smile. "See you tomorrow." And she walked toward the entrance of her home. He could try to stop her, but she certainly wouldn't listen. He was right about one thing. She would no longer be the victim.

Whether James could get past his own demons was a question only he could answer.

Chapter Seven

Under the fluorescent lights of the interrogation room, James glared into Sarah Taylor's blank face. "We have Thomas Bleyer on record saying that you, in fact, did hire him to put out a hit on Lily Reynolds."

With both hands gripping the sides of her chair, she demanded, "I want a lawyer."

Nervous. She might even clam up, but he wasn't too worried. Interrogation was his specialty. "Of course you do. That's all right—you don't have to tell me what I already know, but the judge is going to have a field day with this case. Judge Millman has a particular abhorrence for hitman-for-hire cases."

James watched her dark eyes dart around the room. He tried to suppress the anger he felt toward Sarah for her attempt on Lily's life. Not very professional of him, but he didn't care. Nor would he contain it even if he tried. Instead, he switched gears. She wouldn't talk about the hit, but maybe she would tell him something else useful.

"How long did you know Michael Ronan?"

He saw the sadness wash over her face. She bent forward slightly and let her dark curls fall around her face. "Five years."

"How did you two meet?"

"A friend introduced us. We met at a barbecue."

"What friend?"

"Tina Collins. She owns Innovations Funeral Home on Dillmar Road."

James had to work hard to hide his smile. This was too easy. "Tina introduced the two of you, and then you began dating?"

"Soon after, yes."

"How did Tina know Michael?"

"He was a salesman, working for one of her suppliers. Every year she would have an end-of-summer barbecue and invite her work colleagues and friends. It was a good way for people to network within the mortuary field. Michael really liked Tina. He said he thought she was a smart cookie. They seemed to have had a good working relationship. There may have been a little competition between them but nothing negative that I could tell. Michael loved what he did, and he was really good at it." Her voice cracked on the last word.

James detested Sarah for going after Lily the way she did, but he was also the poster child for understanding what it felt like to lose a loved one. No matter the circumstances, it never felt good. He switched from bad cop to good cop.

"Sarah, we want to catch the person who killed Michael just as much as you, but it doesn't help to have someone take the law into their own hands and potentially harm innocent people."

Her eyes narrowed. "You haven't proven anyone's innocence yet."

"You haven't proven *your* innocence yet either." He turned toward the door, peeled off his suit jacket, and hung it on the doorknob.

She crossed her arms over her chest in a gesture of

defiance. "I want a lawyer."

"Sure, you can have a lawyer, but I was curious about a couple things."

"Such as?" The tone of her voice dropped as if annoyed by his persistence.

James didn't care. He could interrogate her for hours if needed. He didn't need food or water until he got answers. Jimmy once nicknamed him *The Interrogation Machine*.

"How close are you with Tina?"

"I've cut her hair in my house, and we go out from time to time. Her husband passed away not too long ago, so I've really been there for her lately."

"What did he die from?"

"I think from cancer—something terrible."

"Did you know that Michael hung out in a bar called Metal Horse?"

The shift in her eye might have been minute, but James recognized instantly Sarah knew something. "I don't know why he liked that place so much. He went there so often you'd think he was having an affair or something."

"Was he?"

"Not that I know of. He had some creepy friends over there. I never liked going to that bar. Not my scene. Put it this way—they hated everyone. People who hate so much shouldn't be carrying guns."

"Did any of them kill anyone to your knowledge?"

"I have no idea, but I wouldn't be surprised—gives me the chills just talking about it."

"Why do you think he liked going there so much if the patrons are so repulsive?"

"Michael liked motorcycles. He owned one. He felt

like he belonged in that place."

James breathed deeply. Not much to go on but definitely a red flag. He'd have to look at Metal Horse a little closer. "Tell me about the complaint you left at the Reynolds Funeral Home back in March."

She looked alarmed at his abrupt change in subject. "There's not much to tell. I specifically asked for a light wash of color for my mother's face, and Lily made her look like a clown. She also added hydrangeas to the decor of the viewing parlor, and I never asked for them. I detest hydrangeas, and so did my mother."

"So you were upset and decided to call and complain?"

"Yes, I wanted my money back. I didn't get what I asked for, and funerals aren't cheap, you know. There's nothing wrong with that."

"Did they offer you a refund?"

She shook her head. "No, when I booked the job, I had to sign something that said no refunds. Isn't that convenient?"

"I'd imagine it would be hard for them to start over again with your mother. That policy doesn't seem so harsh."

"Sounds like you're defending them."

"So then you proceeded to threaten their business, yell, hang up, and you weren't done there. You hired a hitman for Lily Reynolds."

This time she kept her eyes on his face. "Allegedly."

"Is Tina the one who told you Lily might have murdered Michael?"

"Yes. That greedy animal. All Lily cares about is herself."

"And you believed Tina?"

"Yes, I did. Why shouldn't I?"

"What would be Lily's motive?"

"Retaliation. She was worried I would try to sink her business by reporting her to the state. People take those complaints very seriously. She couldn't stand to lose her livelihood and bring the rest of her family down with her."

"Only if the state thought she was really doing something wrong."

"Ah, she must have hidden things from them. There are probably years of mismanagement going on at Reynolds. The sky's the limit. Has anyone even bothered to check if she's running a legit business? Doesn't anyone ask how they've been open for so long? She's probably selling organs over there."

James scrunched his face. "That's a stretch. Or maybe they run a legit and successful business. I've looked at their records and haven't seen anything out of the ordinary. Only records of your screaming complaints."

Sarah blinked hard, looking annoyed. "Well, someone should look harder."

"In any case, you know that Tina runs a rival business. She has a reason to point the finger at Lily."

"Tina's a good friend. She wouldn't make that up."

"You'd be surprised what a person will do for money."

"Tina is a very savvy businesswoman. She doesn't need to resort to such lowbrow tactics. No, I don't believe she did anything wrong. She's a victim just like myself, and the criminal has to pay."

"Victims don't try to get others killed."

"I want my lawyer."

"I know you do." James was through with her. He walked to the door, replaced his jacket, and knocked to get Jimmy's attention. "See you in court."

****

James glanced at Abrams as they waited at a traffic light on their way to pick up Lily's car from Innovations Funeral Home parking lot. The weight of Abrams's judgment made James uneasy. Don didn't agree with the direction James had taken with the investigation, but he knew deep in his bones that Lily had nothing to do with Ronan's murder. The truth would come out…soon.

"Why did you have to pick her up?"

James fudged the truth. "She said she went to get something from the funeral home, but the manager on duty thought she was a burglar. I gave her a ride home."

"Sounds funny. Don't you think?"

"All of it sounds funny. You've got a rival business owner telling anyone who will listen that her competitor is a murderer. This Tina Collins person sounds like she's hypnotized everyone to believe what she wants them to believe."

"Or it's all true. Have you talked to Tina yet?"

"Not yet."

"Why not?"

"I'm still gathering facts and picking people's brains, but she's looking mighty interesting."

"Or you don't have enough on her."

"I have enough. I'm working on it."

"Seems a bit dramatic, doesn't it? To kill a person to get rid of a business competitor?"

"People have killed for much less."

"True. Who spilled the beans on Tina anyway?"

"Thomas Bleyer."

"The hitman?"

"He's got no reason to lie to me. Definitely worth checking out."

"Did Lily tell you what it was she forgot at Tina's business that caused her to get arrested for burglary?"

"I didn't ask."

"Not very thorough of you. It didn't occur to you to ask that question? You automatically believed her?"

"That's what she told me, but she wasn't there for that reason. I'm sure she went there to find something to incriminate Tina. She's caught on to Tina's role in pointing the finger at her. Doesn't surprise me she would want to look into her."

"So what you're saying is you support her breaking into Tina's house if it means she might find some evidence against Tina."

"Not quite."

Abrams looked over at James as they pulled into the parking lot of Innovations Funeral Home. "Just make sure there isn't another reason why you're keeping Lily off your radar. As far as I'm concerned, she is still our number one suspect."

"I know that."

"And another thing. Don't risk your reputation over a skirt. You're a good detective. I'd hate to see you lose your career over a few bad decisions."

James sighed. "Yes, sir."

He pulled up next to Lily's silver sport coupe and got in.

Abrams took the wheel of James's car and followed him to the Reynolds Funeral Home. A few minutes later, they pulled up to Lily's place. A jittery nervousness came over James. He got that way whenever he was around her. She did something to him that no one else ever had, drawing him in like a magnetic force.

Abrams waited in the car as James stepped out and went up to the house to return her car keys. He knocked at the front door. His nerves made him jumpy. The sun beamed down on his leather jacket, warming his skin. The bright-yellow tulips surrounding the entrance matched the exterior of the house and gave it a cheery appearance—quite the contrast to what went on inside. A minute later, the door opened to Lily, standing there with an apron full of brushes. The red flame of her hair had been tied back out of her face, and her eyes glittered silver in the midday sunlight. His tongue locked up at the sight of her.

"You brought my car. Great. I was about to ask Antonio if I could borrow the hearse to get more face powder. I have to keep a wide range of colors available for my clients, and I seem to be out of the one known as Sand. You want to come in for a minute?"

"Sure." His mouth answered before his brain had time to think. "Just for a minute. Abrams is waiting downstairs in the car."

He stepped in and followed her into the makeup room. But he didn't really care if Abrams waited. That jerk had given him a hard enough time about Lily. Let him stew about it in the car. "I talked to Sarah this morning. She didn't admit to hiring the hitman—that's not so shocking—but she did have a lot to say about Tina Collins and you."

"That's also not so shocking. She's obviously still

pissed about whatever I didn't provide for her mother's viewing, and she's been brainwashed by Tina into thinking I had something to do with her boyfriend's murder. The truth is Tina is jealous. She's mad because her business didn't take off like ours, and she'll keep putting lies into everyone's head to bring us down. But it won't work. We'll be here toiling away while her business tanks."

The flames in her eyes stirred something in him. She was a fighter. He liked that. This was vastly different than what he'd been used to. He was always the protector, and when he'd failed, his world collapsed. Maybe he could get over the fears of his past if he had a strong woman by his side. At least, he wanted to try.

"What else do you know about Tina?"

"I know she's ruthless," Lily said, avoiding eye contact with him.

He could tell she was holding back. "What's wrong?"

"I guess it won't matter if I tell you at this point. In fact, you probably already know what she's been up to. I came upon a photo the other day that fell out of her purse. It proves, without a doubt, there's something up with her."

"You came upon it?" He cocked his head to one side. "Care to elaborate?"

"Shanna and I went to the annual mortuary conference in the City. I happened to run into Tina at one of the workshops. We had an awkward exchange."

"Awkward how?"

Lily stared down at the ground. "I confronted her. I wanted to tell her to stop spreading rumors. I thought maybe if I came at her in person, she'd back down."

"Did she?"

"Not really. But who knows—maybe some of it sunk into her head."

"And the photo?"

She narrowed her eyes at him. "I didn't steal it. The photo dropped out of her bag as she stormed off."

"And you didn't stop her to give it back?"

"Absolutely not." She shook her head. "I need to search for my own evidence."

He raised an eyebrow. Those were the words he wanted to hear the least. "Let's see it."

He watched Lily walk over to a cabinet against the opposite wall. She pulled something out, then held it out to him. "If this doesn't prove she's involved somehow, I don't know what will."

The photo was of a happy couple—Sarah Taylor and Michael Ronan in a romantic embrace. It confused him but did not point him in one direction or the other. "Why would she have this?"

"I'm sure they hung out together, but given everything that's happened, I think it's odd she's carrying around a photo of the two of them in her purse. I think there's something else there."

"Maybe she misses them."

"Maybe she did something terrible and feels really guilty about it."

James breathed heavily through his nose. He had to give her credit for trying. Tina had a motive. "Anything's possible. It's definitely worth checking out." He put his hands in his pockets and shrugged his shoulders. "What are you doing with it? I hope you weren't planning on checking up on her yourself. Or maybe planning another break-in?"

Lily's eyes narrowed; her nostrils flared. "What do you care what I do with it? All this time, you thought I killed him."

"I don't think you did it—"

"Only recently, and I'm not even sure that's really true. There's probably a small part of you that still thinks I may have had something to do with the murder."

"That's totally false. This is about your safety. Lily, it's bad out there. You haven't seen what I've seen. I don't want you running around playing detective and putting yourself in danger."

"Playing detective? I'm trying to save my reputation and my business. I'm not playing detective. I'm the only one I can count on around here. If you and Abrams can't focus on the real killer, then I will."

The door to the makeup room opened abruptly. "What's going on here? What's all the shouting for?" Shanna asked while glancing back and forth from Lily to James.

"Nothing," Lily answered. "We were just talking."

"Didn't sound like talking to me." Shanna stared directly at James. "What's the issue?"

"We were talking about Tina Collins. She's been causing a lot of trouble lately, and I want to get to the bottom of it without having to worry about Lily getting involved and getting hurt."

Shanna chuckled. "Good luck trying to get my sister to do anything she doesn't want to do. Tina needs to be dealt with one way or another, and if you cops aren't going to do something, then we'll be forced to take the law into our own hands. I'm going to leave the two of you to hash it out, but keep it down. I've got a new client interview going on, and I don't want to lose him over your noisy squabble."

Once Shanna was gone, Lily turned her back and began cleaning up her counter space. "I think you should leave, Detective. I've got work to do."

James's heart dropped to his knees. He felt defeated and misunderstood. "That's fine. I'll go if you want, but I'm only trying to keep you safe. I hope you see that."

He reluctantly turned to leave. This had not gone the way he'd wanted. He'd meant to bring her car over and be the hero he was so used to being. He hadn't expected her to be so defiant and stubborn. But he rather her be safe and mad at him than let her win and end up dead at a crime scene. On his way out, he dropped her car keys on the small console table by the front door and walked out into the spring air.

He kicked the tires of his car.

"Everything all right?" Abrams asked, his tone mildly concerned.

"Yes, sir."

He stood there a minute, staring at the Reynolds place. His past haunted him on a daily basis. He wasn't sure if he could ever let it go and allow Lily to be who she was, an independent and perfect woman. But as he gave the place one last look before entering the car, he knew he wanted to try as hard as humanly possible.

Chapter Eight

"That Reynolds brat!" Tina and Chris stared at the graffiti spray-painted on the outside walls of Innovations. The shiny, black lacquered letters of *Killer* and *Rat* stood out like neon signs.

"Call the cops," she snarled. "He can't get away with this."

"How do you know it was Zach?"

"Only Lily Reynolds's little brother would do something so childish. First, she tried to break into Innovations, and now this happens. If Zachary didn't have his family business to fall back on, he'd be locked up in a supermax prison by now. Call the cops. I want that kid to pay for this mess and clean it up, too."

Chris dialed 9-1-1 as they walked back inside.

"Company meeting!" she announced through the house intercom.

She sat at her desk, waiting for her employees to gather. Her blood pressure must be sky-high. She grabbed the white squeeze ball at the corner of her desk. Calming herself down had to be the priority before she cracked skulls. She'd had enough of that Reynolds family. The constant flirting between the desperate single older sister and Donald Abrams made Tina sick. Everyone in town knew his stance on marriage, yet her behavior with him continued. No wonder Lily has been misguided all her life. With no parents, from an early age, she'd had no one to look up to but her tramp of a sister.

After the loss of their parents, Shanna had been forced to take on both raising those two kids and running the family business at a young age. At least Tina had her mother, who'd been strict and set her straight when needed. She'd also taught her how to get what she wanted in life. Shanna, on the other hand, had a reputation for being way too lenient, and Zachary had been a lost cause years ago.

The stories people told about Zachary's bad behavior would make anyone's hair stand up straight. He stole baseball cards from Poster World up the street from the Reynolds's place. One night, he set fire to garbage cans on the playground outside his school. Who does that? A kid with no parents does that, that's who. Lawless and useless.

Marcia strolled in with Simon and Chris trailing behind her. "Something wrong?"

Tina pumped her squeeze ball harder. "Didn't you see the lovely words on the outside of the building?"

Marcia and Simon shared a look. "No, we both got in before sunrise," she said, her voice barely a whisper. "We wanted to get the new equipment you ordered installed before any potential clients walked in."

"Good." Tina released the ball onto her desk. "New equipment might help attract more customers but not with those words slapped across my business.

"What words?" Simon asked.

"Go have a look for yourself. Then, get some linens and drape them across the wall until we can get someone out here to paint over it. Chris, call the painters."

"Who would do this?" Simon chimed in as he replaced his pen into his scrub top pocket.

"The Reynolds family, of course," Tina spat. "They've been after me to close my business for years. They try to act like they don't care about their competition, but that's *all* they care about. I remember when I first opened Innovations, Shanna was so worried about the competition she filed complaints with the historical society, claiming this building sits on top of ancient burial grounds. The historical society dismissed the claims."

"That didn't stop her?" Marcia asked.

Tina grinned. "What Shanna didn't know is that I already had secured the permits to open the business and was not planning on disturbing the grounds anyway. What a joke."

"That's embarrassing," Chris said. "Did she apologize?"

"She tried to do all this secretly. To this day, she isn't aware that I know she was the one who filed the claim."

"Not a good start to your relationship."

"No, it wasn't. They initiated the quarrel, not me. Ever since then, I've had to constantly watch my back."

"I've heard they're perpetually arguing," Chris said. "You'd think they'd hire outside help with all that internal drama going on."

"They won't let anyone outside the family come to work for them," Tina said. "They're like a cult, especially that weirdo Zachary. He's part owner but barely does anything. You'd think he'd realize stuff like this puts their business on the hot seat."

Chris said, "Definitely not good for business."

Tina scooped up the squeeze ball again. Her fingers worked overtime, putting all her aggression into the malleable surface. "Lily's no angel either. She secretly resents Shanna for inheriting more control of the business. As she's gotten older, I've watched her want to branch out and be her own person. She tried doing some freelance makeup on the side for a while, but that didn't last long. Her technique was fine, but she didn't find the work satisfying. So she quit."

Chris tilted his head to one side. "That's not so terrible."

"She's been pretty straight-edge—until now. She's got her own drama going on."

"Which is?"

"She's dating that new detective when there's a murder case going on, and she's a possible suspect. Talk about a scandal."

"That means the detectives probably don't think she did it," Simon chimed in.

"Well, that's absurd. She may be straight-edged, but everyone knows she's a hothead with a hair-trigger temper. She'd be the first on my list."

Chris stared at Tina. "But could she kill a person?"

Tina felt her face turn to stone. "To save everything a person has ever worked for? Absolutely." She could relate.

The sound of a car pulling up outside meant the police had arrived—music to Tina's ears. After taking a deep cleansing breath, she stood. "Let's all get back to work. I'll handle the cops."

She walked out of her office toward the front door. When she opened the door, her face fell. Dressed in a sharp navy suit with a burgundy tie peeking out from behind the police badge hanging from his neck, Detective James Rivers sauntered up her front steps.

She crossed her arms in disgust. "You. I'm looking for the real cops, not a fresh one full of bias and inexperience."

"I'm as real as they get," James replied. "What seems to be the problem here, Ms. Collins?"

"You call yourself a detective? Can't you see for yourself?" she yelped, gesturing at the graffiti-covered walls. "Your girlfriend's bratty brother vandalized my place of business. He needs to be taken into custody immediately."

His mouth curved into a smirk. "As a matter of fact, I did see the writing. I thought maybe you were redecorating or something."

His lack of professionalism confirmed her negative theories about him. "You would. You ignored that Lily Reynolds tried to break into Innovations. This time are you going to arrest Zachary or stand there trying to be funny? I should report you."

"That's not how it works, Ms. Collins. I don't have any proof Zachary Reynolds did anything. In fact, I'd like to come in and talk. Maybe we can get down to why you think he would vandalize your property."

She stood firm in front of her door, hoping he'd take the hint. "I don't need a detective for that. Why don't you go arrest him already and stop wasting time?"

"I'd like to speak with you for a few moments inside—call it a formality."

Tina sighed. She didn't have the energy to fight him. But she also had no faith that letting him in would help her. She had to take control of this visit. In her mind, if the Reynolds family business continued to exist, there would be no chance that Innovations would ever succeed. Not to mention the incredible anger Tina had been holding onto her whole life for the death of her father, which she attributed to the Reynolds. On top of that, Chris told her Lily tried to break into Innovations. If Tina played her cards right, this would be a good opportunity to get Detective Rivers behind her cause and smash the Reynolds family for good. She stood to the side, allowing him into the house.

"This is a very modern facility—quite different from the Reynolds place," he said with a nod for her two favorite Pop Art paintings in the foyer. She preferred clean lines and her workspace uncluttered.

"We pride ourselves in being state-of-the-art for those who want a modern touch to their loved ones' for the viewing. We have the most up-to-date caskets," she said, leading him into their sales room where the casket samples were kept. "You can have any theme you want painted on your coffin, done by our very own staff member, Marcia Alonso. The American flag is one we get requests for all the time. We can even customize the shape. People like the car-shaped one quite a bit, and we can even do one out of clear acrylic if you want to see the deceased through the sides.

The detective bit his lip and quickly backed away from the display. "That's…strange."

"We don't judge here. We are very open-minded and anti-tradition."

"Sounds like you've really differentiated yourself from the basic funeral home."

"That's right. I have, and don't even get me started on our state-of-the-art embalming system. I recently acquired equipment that works so efficiently we can cut down our embalming time and schedule the viewing sooner than the average funeral home. The clients get what they want and can move through the grieving process faster."

He rubbed his chin and then cleared his throat. "Sounds like the perfect choice for someone looking for…services." He turned to her. "Tell me one thing, why isn't your business thriving? I've made it a point to drive by Innovations a couple times over the last few days—at different hours. I didn't see the parking lot filled with cars at any of my drive-bys. Why don't I see more action here?"

Tina pressed her lips together into a thin, hard line. Who was he to judge her brilliant business plan? He was the one letting the Reynolds family run amok. "This is a small town, Detective. People struggle with change. All the Reynolds had to do was sit back and carry on the legacy while I had to build mine from the ground up."

"Mind if I have a look around?"

Tina hesitated. She didn't want Detective Bozo rifling through her things, but she also didn't want him to think she had anything to hide. "Briefly. I don't want to share my company secrets."

"I'll be sure to avert my eyes if I get too close to those secrets." Rivers left the sales room and walked toward the embalming room. Tina followed closely behind to keep tabs on him.

"Detective Rivers, nice to meet you."

She overheard him introduce himself to Simon and didn't bother following him into the embalming room. Simon would only be cleaning and testing the new equipment, the cop wouldn't find anything in there.

A few minutes later, Rivers came back out and headed toward a closed door opposite the embalming room. "What's in here?"

Tina lingered in the hallway. "Makeup room."

After he knocked on the door, Marcia let him in. Tina heard a similar exchange occur between the two. Hopefully, Marcia wouldn't sink this ship. Her timid nature would never convince the cop of her company's innocence. But he would find the same thing in the makeup room as he did in the embalming room—nothing.

Before her next negative thought, Rivers came out of the makeup room. His face appeared a bit forlorn. Good.

"What's upstairs?" He pointed toward the narrow staircase.

"My bedroom and a second bedroom I converted into a library. There's nothing up there to see either."

He started up the steps. "I'll just take a quick peek if you don't mind, then be on my way."

"Is that really necessary? The vandalism occurred outside. I doubt Zachary even stepped foot inside."

Rivers turned back to her. "I'm being thorough. When I arrived earlier, you said you wanted a real cop, not an inexperienced one. Didn't you?"

"Maybe I did." She giggled in her head. Sometimes even she couldn't believe what came out of her mouth.

"I want you to trust that I've responded to your complaint and put in the work my superiors expect from me. It's my job to see if anything was left behind or vandalized. You're welcome to come up with me. I'll only be a few seconds. Will you consent to my search upstairs?"

"Make it quick. I need to get back to work. This stuff doesn't pay for itself," Tina announced at his back. She felt pretty confident he wouldn't find anything. Despite his explanations, he didn't seem thorough at all. Amateur. The whole town knew Abrams was the real detective on the Manorview force. Who was this clown anyway? He comes into town and immediately gets assigned the Ronan case? Had he even proven himself enough to get the town's one and only murder case in the last five years? Then he tries to bed Lily Reynolds without even considering what that would do to his reputation. Crazy.

Tina walked to the bottom of the stairs, stretching her neck to look for him. "All set?" she yelled up the stairs.

His voice trailed back down. "Yes."

"We really need to get to work now, Detective," she announced again. Nervous energy made her hands sweat. What was he into up there?

Just as she put one foot on the first step, Rivers appeared at the top of the stairs.

"All set. Thank you for cooperating. We'll be in touch regarding the vandalism." He glided down the stairs past her. The look on his face seemed less confused and more purposeful as he rushed toward the entry door.

"See that you do. I want Zachary Reynolds to pay for the repairs, and it's clear to me his family is targeting my business. Anyone can see that. Will you choose to do something about it is the real question," she barked at his back.

"I'll be in touch soon," he said again and let the front door swing closed behind him.

Tina's mouth hung open, dumbfounded.

"What was that about?" Chris asked as he approached her from the office.

"Amateurs," Tina spat.

****

"Why did you do that?" Lily shouted.

Zachary shoved a ham and cheese sandwich in his mouth. "She needs to pay. I'm tired of sitting back while that Collins bitch makes all of our lives suck."

"Great. She'll for sure call the cops on you. Then what? You want to spend time behind bars? And how does that help the business that you say you care so much about?"

"Yeah, Zach," Shanna chimed in as she leaned against the doorway in the lounge, watching her siblings bicker. "Makes no sense."

"She deserved it," he replied.

"And I'm sure she will retaliate." Lily's mind raced with the possibilities. "It's just a matter of time."

Rising from the table, Zachary threw the rest of the sandwich in the trash. "I can't believe the two of you think it's perfectly fine for Tina to convince our vendors to stop selling stuff to us. You guys might be all right with her big mouth, but I'm not going to sit around and take it." He stormed out of the lounge.

Lily looked at her sister.

"Hard to argue with that," Shanna said.

"Oh, sure. Defend him. Two vendors. That's all we lost." Lily put up two fingers. "It won't break us. If it were Embalmer Warehouse, I'd be more worried. But one caterer and a lone flower supplier are easily replaceable."

"Embalmer Warehouse has been loyal for years,"

Shanna said. "No loose-lipped, unsuccessful, jealous business person is going to change our relationship with them."

"But it doesn't excuse Zachary's behavior," Lily said. "He can't go vandalizing people's homes, no matter how awful they are."

"I agree, but he's always going to do what he wants. Maybe she won't press charges."

Lily glared at her.

"Cops are here!" Zachary shouted as he ran out of the house. "I'm outta here."

Shanna sighed. "I'm stepping out, too. I think I've had enough drama to fill a lifetime. Plus, Don Abrams won't come out for graffiti. It'll be James. You've got to convince him to look closer at Tina. We've been under attack by her, and it's time to stop her."

"Have you talked to Abrams?" Lily asked.

"We went out for dinner the other night. I confronted him about his finger-pointing at you. I asked him how he could do such a thing. He assured me they were looking at other suspects, and you were off their radar."

"Did you yell at him?"

"I sure did."

"Did you sleep with him?"

Shanna's mouth dropped open. "Lily!"

"He accused me of murder. I would think that might stop you."

"Don't you think I know that?

"He apologized—"

"Not to me."

"He will, I promise. He's a good man and a brilliant detective, but he made a mistake here. Even I wanted to know what he really thought about the case, but he was fairly tight-lipped about it. It sounded like James has been keeping some of his investigation to himself. I got the sense there was tension between him and Donnie."

"I'm sure *Donnie* doesn't like to be proven wrong. As a newcomer to town, James needs to tread lightly. But I think he'll tear Abrams's theory apart."

At the knock on the front door, Shanna stood. "I'll see you later. Be careful," she said, leaving through the back door.

Lily approached the front door, chest out, defenses up. Zachary was guilty. He had committed a crime, but with every fiber of her being, she would try to talk James out of arresting him.

She opened the door to a completely different James Rivers. His eyes gleamed with delightful mischief. The smile on his face made her heart pound. The word *gorgeous* came to mind. She was supposed to be mad at him for treating her like a damsel in distress. Her life history didn't allow her to be saved by anyone, and she wasn't going to start now. But that smile.

Something had happened since the last time he'd been here. Something good.

"Is this about Tina?"

He nodded. "I need to tell you what I've discovered."

"He's just a kid, James. I'm sure you've got bigger things to worry about than some graffiti on a wall. In fact, I'm shocked you're even here at all."

He shook his head. "That's not why I'm here." He let himself in, shut the door behind him, and stood very close to her—closer than he'd been in a while.

103

An avalanche of nerves flooded her system. She couldn't think straight. She should kick him out. Get rid of him before he talked about the vandalism. Instead, she stood there absorbing him, torn between her attraction to him and the loyalty to her family.

"Tina called the station to report the vandalism. I went over there and convinced her to consent to a search so that I wouldn't have to get a warrant. Everything checked out until I went into her bedroom. Hidden under clothing in her dresser was a letter from Michael Ronan."

Lily's stomach flipped. Words refused to form in her mouth.

"I found a love letter," he said. " That means they were having an affair. This case could simply be a lover's quarrel. Maybe she wanted him to leave Sarah, and he refused. Tina went into a jealous rage and killed him. Then she dumped the body here and used Sarah to pin it on you, damage your reputation, and drive your customers to her."

Lily reached up to hug him. "Finally."

She closed her eyes and smiled for the first time in a very long time. "This is amazing. I'm so relieved!"

He raised up out of the hug but kept his arms around her. "I need to apologize, Lily. I've been so caught up in the pressure to solve the case that I haven't treated you fairly. Believe me, I didn't want to be so rough on you, but Abrams kept pushing me in one direction when my gut told me something else."

Lily's heart swelled. To admit he'd been wrong could not have been easy. "Apology accepted."

He took in a deep breath. "And I promise to focus all of my efforts toward the right people and not get influenced by Abrams."

She could tell this was hard for him.

"I'll try to let go as much as possible. I can't say that it'll be perfect or that I won't have a strong reaction to want to keep you safe, but...I'm trying."

"I know you are." Lily rested her chin on his chest, thinking they hadn't had a proper kiss. The last time they'd been in this position, he'd pulled away from her. His past had been a constant intrusion, holding him back from living his life. This she understood completely.

He leaned toward her, letting his lips land on hers. This kiss felt more deliberate, thoughtful, and gentle. Not too much, not too little. Just enough to show his affection and appreciation but nothing more. It was a small step for them, but at least for now, neither pulled away. This kiss felt real, comforting, one filled with promise. Shivers ran up and down her spine. The pounding in her ears was all she could hear.

Finally.

This time Lily pulled away, not because she wanted the kiss to end, but she couldn't resist the opportunity to tease him.

"Since I'm such a good detective, maybe I should quit the funeral business and come work with you."

James's shoulders went up. "Uh, I don't know if that's such a good idea. I think—"

"The case wouldn't have been solved without me, and you know it. I could share desk space with you. We could go to lunch and discuss our theories."

"I think you're great at your creepy day job—"

Lily grinned. "You could put in the paperwork for me to get my own gun."

When James's face fell she knew she'd gone over the edge. "Too far?"

"Now you're pushing it."

Chapter Nine

James walked into Old Town Bar. He'd heard from some of the guys at the station that Don Abrams had spent the last several hours here—in broad daylight. When he'd arrived in the parking lot, he had to shield his eyes from the blinding sun. Once he got inside, the vibe was dank and gloomy, no doubt to hide the vices lurking within. James spotted Abrams in a corner booth, slouched over a glass containing a mixture of melted ice and his drink of choice—probably scotch.

He slid onto the vinyl bench seat. "Thought I would find you here. The boys at the station said this is where you've been spending a lot of your time."

"Did you come to gloat?" Abrams said into his glass—barely enunciating his words.

"No, I came as a friend." James glanced around—not too many people drinking today. *Good.* He didn't want Abrams to become the talk of the town.

"You call stealing the case of a lifetime something a friend would do? Do you know how long it takes to get a case like this in a small town? No, you wouldn't. You've barely started your career."

"I didn't steal your case. I did the right thing."

"The right thing? You never discussed what you knew about Tina Collins with me. You kept it all to yourself so that you can call yourself the winner."

"There are no winners here, Don."

"Of course there are. How do you think I got the reputation I have in this town? You think it just comes to you with time? No, you've got to prove yourself."

"And you have. Everyone knows that. Why are you so stuck on this case?"

"James, haven't I taught you anything? The people in this town trust me. They know at the end of the day, their hero, Detective Don Abrams, will be there to solve the case. They can go ahead and rest their heads at night, knowing I'm out there patrolling the street for the bad guys in their nightmares."

"And they will still feel that way—"

"I remember the day I solved my first murder case in Manorview. Almost thirty years ago. The killer sneaked into the homes of young women, strangling them in their beds. The media dubbed him the Night Strangler. For months this guy terrorized the whole town. No one knew when he would strike again. People went out and bought expensive alarm systems and big attack dogs to warn them of anyone approaching their houses at night."

"So how did you catch him?"

"I got lucky. One night one of his victims fought back. He left behind some blood, and the woman he attacked lived to give a physical description. Back then, we didn't have DNA testing, like we do now, but I put him in a lineup, and the victim identified him. When we put him away, it was probably one of the happiest days of my life. I felt powerful knowing I helped bring peace back to Manorview. Mayor Gunthall came to personally thank me. People talked about that case for weeks."

"You were considered a hero."

"That's right."

"And now you feel that the town will forget about that case and you."

Abrams didn't answer, but his eyes welled up with tears.

James leaned across the table. "It's not going to happen. This town will always respect you the way you deserve. I guarantee it. That is, except for today. Drinking in this bar—not your best day."

Abrams lifted and then slammed his glass down. "And how do you think this looks to Shanna?"

"Since when do you care so much what she thinks?"

Abrams chuckled. "You think I don't have a heart. boy?"

James's mouth dropped open in disbelief. "Well, well. The most famous detective in all the land is in love?"

A smirk appeared on his face. He took a long swig of his drink to hide it.

"When did this happen?"

James casually turned his head toward the clanging of ice coming from a martini shaker at the bar. He watched the bartender pour out the brown liquid into a tall glass in front of an older-looking lady with frizzy white curls and a burgundy tracksuit. She had a lit cigarette dangling out of the corner of her mouth as she talked to the bartender.

"Shanna and I have been getting closer recently."

James turned his attention back to Abrams. "Even though you've been pointing the finger at Lily?"

"She didn't know the details of the case, only heard the rumors."

"Still, it's her sister."

"Geez, I told her I was sorry. And I've backed off on Lily."

"I'd still be mad at you."

"She probably is. But that's not your problem. In fact, you have no problems whatsoever because you're the best. You got to the answer before I did, and now you are the hero." He raised his glass, gave the contents a swirl. "Congratulations."

"Tell you what, why don't you make the arrest? I don't need the glory. You can be the one to put Tina in your vehicle for all to see. Would that make things better?"

Abrams slammed the glass down. "Are you mocking me?"

"No, I'm trying to make it better. What can I do?"

"It's too late. The boys think I'm a failure. Thirty-five years of service has come down to this."

"I think you're being dramatic. Your reputation is still intact. So you didn't get this one case. Big deal."

"That's what you don't get. It's a very big deal."

"Abrams, the only person to blame is yourself. If you hadn't been stuck on the wrong suspect for so long, you would've nailed this one."

"Who do you think you are talking to? I gave you everything you have in this town, boy. If it weren't for me, you'd still be back in the City battling drunks and drug addicts." Abrams stood up out of the booth and puffed up his chest.

"You have no idea what you are talking about." James also stood up to meet him, although slightly awkward since Abrams towered over him. "I've paid s If anything, it's the opposite. You've done nothing but obstruct the Ronan case." James pointed at Abrams's chest, no doubt infuriating him even more.

"Obstruct?" Abrams's eyes narrowed to pinpoints. "The only obstruction was you and that Lily tramp. No wonder you didn't want me to pursue her. You were too busy trying to get her into the sack."

James's mind went blank. No thoughts. Pure reaction. The right hook swing connected with Abrams's chin and brought him crashing down. He immediately regretted it but at the same time couldn't stop himself. The anger coursing through his veins had taken over his body.

Abrams struggled to get up. He'd had too much to drink to fight back. His response was too slow and too stunted for retaliation.

The bouncer rushed over, creating a barrier between the men. His large body blocked any view James had of Abrams. "You two are out. Let's go." He shoved James toward the exit, which was fine with him. He'd caused enough problems and just wanted to leave at this point. Abrams would have to sleep it off.

Abrams finally staggered out of the bar, squinting in the daylight. Without the darkness of the bar to hide all of his problems, he looked downright pathetic as he tried to put one foot in front of the other and failing miserably.

But James was not a heartless man. He helped Abrams up and let him hang on until they reached James's car. "You're going to hate yourself in the morning," he told him as he helped him into the passenger side.

Abrams held the side of his face. "I already do."

James drove toward Abrams's apartment building.

He saw his boss's eye had already begun to close from the swelling, but that didn't stop him from wanting to talk.

"Take back what you said about Lily."

"Not a chance."

James stomped so hard on the brakes, Abrams's face crashed against the glove compartment. "Okay, okay. I take it back. Quit beating me up while I'm intoxicated. You have an unfair advantage."

James resumed driving. "Good. Keep telling yourself that."

"What I want to know is what happened to your never-dating-again policy?" Abrams asked. He made a motion with his tongue like he was checking to see if all his teeth were still in place.

"I guess the policy changed."

"Seems so. I had no idea how deep it went."

"How deep what went?"

"You and Lily."

He had a good point. James had not expected to get violent in her defense. He had not seen it coming either. There was no way out now, even if he wanted it. He'd let her in, though he had promised never to put himself in a position where someone could get hurt. He had failed.

"Neither did I."

Chapter Ten

Gina's Beauty Bazaar was one of Lily's favorite places. Located on Sharon Road, it took only minutes to get there when she needed to bulk up on supplies or get away for a bit of browsing. Aisle after aisle, beauty products were lined up on the shelves as far as the eye could see—shampoo, hair dyes, brushes, makeup tools, accessories. You name it, Gina's probably had it, and Lily knew the owner pretty well. She spent so much time there she received automatic discounts on all her purchases.

This morning she'd gone out for makeup brush cleaner. Lord knows she went through buckets of the stuff since she had to clean them after every client. The big blue liquid bottles were the best—the ones you dunked the brushes in and instantly they'd be clean. No muss. No fuss. As she walked into the store, she made a beeline for the third aisle where she would find those precious bottles.

Lily stood in front of a sea of blue bottles, ready to pluck a few off the shelf, when she overheard whispering. Not the super-quiet kind of whispering, but the kind you can understand from a few feet away.

"What about the younger one in the funeral parlor. The one who gets around?"

"Lily? I heard she's dating the cops."

"All of them?"

"At least the new guy."

"The one on the Ronan murder case?"

"If she's banging the main detective on the case, that would certainly get her out of trouble."

Great. That's what people thought of her? Nothing but a floozy?

Giggling came from the other side of the aisle. Her heart sank. She didn't recognize the voices, but clearly, people were gossiping about her. "Yeah, that's convenient. Wish I could get away with murder, too. My husband would be the first to go."

When loud, raucous laughter exploded from the other side of the aisle, all the air blew out of Lily's lungs like a deflated tire. Why were people so cruel? Joking about her relationship was one thing. To make fun of someone being murdered seemed too much.

She lost interest in shopping. In fact, she wanted to get home and sulk in peace. She left the brush cleansers behind, kept her head down, and walked out of the store. She didn't even bother stopping by the counter to say hello to Gina. Humiliation won this time.

She'd return to her job and lay low for a while until she and James figured out what they were, and the Ronan case could finally be put to rest. Were they a couple? Not officially, but the rumors would continue until they declared themselves to the world. Until then, she'd go undercover.

Back at the funeral home, Lily stood over the stainless steel sink, cleaning her makeup brushes with the last bit of cleanser she had left. She watched the runoff change from brown to pink to clear as she cleaned each brush. She enjoyed the process. It felt peaceful. Despite the few true haters who held onto rumors and lies, she had much to be thankful for. The last several weeks had completely turned her life on its head. She'd gone from being the number one suspect in a murder to being cleared from any wrongdoing. Her relationship with James was an unexpected bonus, whether they figured out what they wanted or not.

A knock on the door brought her back to the present. Shanna was home but still lingering in her bed as she typically did on Saturday mornings. She would most likely not be up yet. Lily liked to get up early and get things done. She dried her hands on a towel and walked out of the makeup room. Swinging the front door open in her usual carefree manner, she came face to face with the barrel of a gun.

Behind the gun stood a scowling Tina Collins.

"Don't scream. If you do, you're dead," she said, gesturing with the gun. "Get inside."

Lily's heart slammed against her chest as she slowly took a few steps backward into the foyer. This couldn't be the way she died—in her own funeral home. She'd pictured something less dramatic, maybe in her bed surrounded by her kids.

"Why are you doing this?" Lily said it louder than normal. She wanted Shanna to hear her and maybe call James or Abrams.

"I've had just about enough of you." She shook the gun toward the viewing room. "Go in there. I want to be able to put you in one of your own caskets after I kill you. You get to choose which one you prefer." A crooked smile appeared on her face. She seemed perfectly delighted by the idea.

Lily's brain went into overdrive. She'd have to stall and pray Shanna had heard her. "I'm not sure how we got off to such a bad start. I like you. I think your business is innovative and different. There's room for both of us to exist. We can help each other thrive."

"It's too late for all that. You know too much. Your amateur boyfriend has been snooping around, and I don't like it. I'm not ashamed about dating Michael. He loved me more than that whiny hairdresser. There's no question about that. But he knew she would be devastated if he left her for me. He didn't want to deal with that."

"You didn't get what you wanted, so you killed him?" As soon as the words left her mouth, Lily regretted it. Why couldn't she control herself?

"You have never felt that kind of humiliation," Tina whined, cocking the gun. "Not with that red hair and slim body. You've never been rejected as much as I have. Men have thrown themselves at you all your life, so don't judge me. Sooner or later, everyone gets what they deserve. Even you."

Sweat dripped down Lily's chest. A surreal, out-of-body feeling came over her as her mind went blank. Was she not reacting because she had finally resigned herself to die? It seemed like an easier option than constantly battling with Tina and her demons as well. She might even see her parents again in the afterlife. That wouldn't be so bad. Would it?

"I'll be there soon, Mom and Dad," she mumbled.

"What was that? Mom and Dad? Yes, you will see them soon, and while you're there, tell your dad he's a real asshole for putting my father in the clink. Your parents deserved what they got. An eye for an eye. I just wish Dad hadn't turned the gun on himself after. He was misunderstood but a good man. He knew he'd never get out of prison, so he chose to end it all, and now you'll pay for your father's mistakes."

A searing migraine pounded away at Lily's skull as she tried to process what Tina had revealed. All those years she'd wondered about the man who'd slaughtered her family. Rick Johnson. She'd searched the Internet, but the details of his personal life were never revealed. She knew his criminal record by heart and watched reenactments of the night on the news, but she didn't know it had all come down to Tina. Her father had killed Lily's parents for putting him in prison, and then he killed himself immediately after.

And here she stood before her, looking for vengeance. It had all been about getting vengeance for her father? Michael Ronan ended up in her basement to satisfy her need for revenge? Tina had used Sarah's anger toward Lily and got the whole town thinking Lily had killed Ronan. All for vengeance and greed.

A loud smash rang out from the foyer. Tina jumped out of her skin. The jolt of her hand gave Lily enough time to knock her arm away and run across the room. The gun dropped, and Tina tumbled over from the momentum. James barreled into the room, gun in firing position, aimed at Tina. From the floor, she stared with a wide-eyed expression.

She snickered. "I knew you were an amateur. She did all the work for you."

"Only a crazy person would find this moment funny," James replied.

"I am crazy. Crazy-smart enough to fool a whole town. Although it didn't take much to fool you since you're such a newbie."

James leaned over her. Lily saw his jaw grind in

anger from across the room.

"And you'll be going exactly where your father went—prison. For the rest of your life."

Lily watched the smile disappear from Tina's face. But the commotion of backup arriving helped alleviate the tension in the room. A swarm of cops rushed in.

She recognized Michael and Joe, the officers who'd been outside Sarah's house. They both gave her a quick nod before heading over to Tina. They lifted her up off the floor and handcuffed her. As soon as Lily heard the grinding sound of the handcuffs closing around Tina's wrists, she breathed again—a moment she thought would never come.

While they escorted Tina from the scene, Abrams sauntered into the room. Lily noticed the bruise near his left eye. "Everyone all right?" he asked, looking back and forth between them.

James looked at Lily as he replaced his gun in its holster. He looked like he hadn't taken a breath in a very long time.

Physically, she felt fine. Mentally, not so much. "I'm all right. I'm happy it's over."

James came over and embraced her. "It's definitely over. You're free."

Grinning from ear to ear, Lily enjoyed the safety of his arms for a few seconds. The uncertainty of their relationship weighed heavily on her mind, but in this moment, she would gladly lean on him for support. Was she free, though? She had to live with what Tina had told her. The feud between their families. The nature of everyone's death—so violent and sad.

She stared up at James. This incident was a perfect example of why she shouldn't date cops, but as she fell into the comforting depths of his blue eyes, none of that mattered. She hadn't listened to her own advice and may now forever regret that decision.

"Well, you two," Abrams began, his head slightly bowed, "I should apologize first to you, Lily, for maintaining your guilt for so long and then to you, James, for not listening when you told me she had nothing to do with the murder. It wasn't personal."

James looked at Lily. He seemed to want her to have the apology.

"It wasn't an easy case. Tina didn't have *killer* written across her forehead. No one would've suspected her, which was part of her strategy, I guess." She patted James on the back. "Credit goes to him for thinking outside the box."

James smiled sheepishly.

"I think it was more than that, but you're right—he should get the credit," Abrams replied.

"Is everyone all right?" Shanna poked her head around the corner from the bottom of the staircase.

"Yes, thanks to you. I'm assuming you called James when you heard us talking down here?" Lily asked.

"Oh, I definitely heard you two. Truly chilling confession from her. She must've known I'd be home. I figured she'd probably shoot both of us if I showed my face."

"She knew you'd be here. She was going to march right upstairs after she shot me and get you too. I'm glad you didn't come down here."

"Not only did she murder Michael Ronan in cold blood—the man she was supposedly in love with—but then decides she's going to pin it on you to avenge her father. To think all these years we had no idea her father killed our parents. How often had I passed her by at the coffee shop and had no idea she was hiding this secret from us?"

"She must've been embarrassed growing up. Her father's choices aren't her fault, but how she chose to deal with it got her into trouble," James added.

"She killed the man she loved," Lily said, her eyes avoiding James. "How sad."

"She didn't really love him. She couldn't handle losing him to Sarah. Her inability to cope with the loss of her father culminated in her inability to deal with any other type of loss. Her loss in love. Her loss in her business. She had to regain control somehow, and that was going to be achieved through you," James said, staring at Lily.

"Whoa. That was deep. I knew I hired you for a reason," Abrams said, slapping James on the back.

"Detective Rivers must've been a psych major," Shanna quipped.

While the others joked, Lily's heart ached. She didn't want to say anything out loud, but his explanation confirmed why she had broken all her rules and became involved with him. His explanation explained why she had fallen in love with him.

"In any case, I'm happy to say it's over, and we can all move on with our lives," James added.

"Hear, hear." Shanna clapped her hands. "And good riddance. We should celebrate."

"How about a drink later tonight?" James asked.

"Perfect."

****

Old Town Bar had its usual crowd that night. The

Saturday-evening folks were truly happy by the time they arrived, and the regulars had settled in for the long haul.

James breathed a sigh of relief as he approached a corner booth with Lily, Abrams, and Shanna. The standoff with Tina had wiped him out and made him exceptionally hungry. Nothing beat a burger and a beer after catching the bad guy and knowing your girl was safe. James glanced at Lily. Glowing skin, pink lips, and silver-green eyes made his stomach ache, but her occasional yawn and droopy posture meant she was also exhausted. He couldn't contain the gut-wrenching thought of not having her here with him from creeping into his mind. A flash of his lifeless girlfriend lying in his arms sent a shiver through him.

"What's wrong?" Lily asked.

"Absolutely nothing. I'm great." He rubbed her arm. But he wasn't sure if he was all right. Would he ever be all right?

"He should be great. Case closed, and no one on our side died," Abrams bellowed. "That's a good day in my book."

"I missed the punch line," Shanna said. "James, how did you subdue the evil queen?"

James looked at Lily again. She'd been strong and courageous. Was that what he needed? Someone who could clearly take care of herself? "Before I had a chance to disarm her, Lily had knocked the gun out of her hand."

"Oh, now the truth comes out," Abrams interjected. "Who's the *real* hero?"

James glared at him.

"Well, it doesn't surprise me that Lily took matters

into her own hands—danger and all," Shanna said. "When Lily was eighteen, she wanted to explore career options other than being a mortician. That summer, she thought she wanted to try her hand at being a firefighter. She spent one day in the trenches at the local fire station and came home smelling like a dirty sock. That night she crawled on her knees to her bedroom."

"All right, so I hadn't thought that one through, but I learned a lot about communication and teamwork."

James kneaded her shoulder as the waitress came over to their table.

"Good evening, folks. Can I take your order?"

"Hey, Shelley," James greeted her.

Everyone knew Shelley. She'd worked at Old Town Bar all her life and recently celebrated her sixtieth birthday. "Detective." She nodded her head at him. "What'll it be?" she asked in between her gum chewing.

"IPA, and the double-stacked burger with fries."

Shelley didn't bother writing anything down. She nodded and looked at Lily.

Lily glanced at James. "Hungry?"

"Starving."

"You know what? I'll have the same," she replied.

"That's my girl," James said, putting his arm around her.

"We'll both have IPA on tap," Abrams said, ordering for Shanna.

Shelley nodded and walked away.

"The fact that you disarmed Tina is pretty impressive, and you've never worked in law enforcement before?" Abrams asked.

"Ha, very funny," Lily replied.

"No, I'm serious. We could use someone with guts and determination. You could be our case consultant for the precinct. Off the record, of course."

"Now, wait a minute. She's busy running a business, and I don't like the danger you'd be putting her in," Shanna scolded him.

"I agree. Sounds dangerous. We can't ask her to put herself in the lion's mouth. I don't stand by this at all," James added, staring everyone in the eye to make sure they knew he meant business. She'd been able to take care of herself, but he couldn't live with himself if something happened to her. He'd be back to constantly worrying about her safety. *Nope*. This would not fly.

"No one said she had to quit the business. She can help us part time. We'll save the really gut-wrenching cases for her," Abrams continued.

James noted the wicked smile Abrams had developed during the conversation. No doubt he enjoyed watching James squirm.

"Do I get a say?" Lily interjected.

"Of course you do," Shanna added.

Lily sat up straight as if filled with renewed energy. "It's not a terrible idea. I think I can add something to your cases, and it would also mean I could work closer with James. I can still work at the funeral home if I'm super-efficient. I want in."

The look of longing she gave him made his heart sink. How could he say no? He decided to say nothing and rub her leg in solidarity. They'd discuss it again later in private. He would remind her of his past and how hard it would be for him to stomach this.

"He's right to be hesitant on this," Shanna said. "It

might be harder to deal with than you think, Lily. Although, I've got to say I'm a little jealous. You know I like a good crime scene."

"When have you ever been at a crime scene?"

"I watch a lot of true crime shows. That has to count for something, doesn't it?"

"Not really," Lily replied. "But if it makes you feel better, I'll let you read some of my case files." She winked at her sister.

"Deal."

****

Later that night, after dinner, James drove Lily home. Abrams and Shanna stayed behind at the bar a little longer, but she insisted on getting home at a decent hour.

"You're mad?" she asked him as they walked toward her front door.

"Not mad. Worried."

"Listen, I'll be fine. I can take care of myself. You've seen that already. You've got to let it go."

James breathed deeply. He wanted to believe everything was going to be fine. He wanted to move on without anything holding them back, but he wasn't sure he could. "I'm trying. And you suddenly have gotten over your fear of dating cops?"

"No, it's the worst idea I've ever had. It goes against what any rational person would do, but the heart wants what it wants. On some level, I'm starting to feel like the more I fight it, the more I get pushed into the world of law enforcement. Maybe it's in my blood and fighting it would be futile."

"Sounds like you're not giving me a choice in the matter."

"Guess not." Lily moved to put the key in the lock but noticed the door was slightly ajar. "What the heck?" She pushed the door open. "Oh, God!"

James pushed the door open farther.

Lying in a pool of blood was Zachary.

Chapter Eleven

Lily raced to her brother's side and kneeled over him. His eyelids fluttered as they struggled to stay open. "He's still alive. Zachary, stay with me."

She heard James calling for an ambulance, then backup. She checked Zachary's body and found several stab wounds oozing blood. She took off her jacket and used it to apply pressure on them.

She leaned close to his ear. "Who did this to you?"

His mouth moved, but no sound came out. She'd have to trust he'd tell them later, after the people at the hospital stabilized him. She would not let him die here on the floor without a serious fight.

Eight agonizing minutes went by before she heard the sirens of the arriving ambulance. A team of paramedics, hauling a stretcher and massive toolbox, rushed in. Working quickly but efficiently, one EMT connected her brother to a cardiac monitor while the other took Zachary's vital signs and placed a couple IV lines. As both worked, they asked questions—which, of course, her brother was unable to answer. Lily supplied personal information such as blood type, drug allergies, and medical history. As they secured Zachary to the stretcher, Lily felt James's arm around her shoulder.

"He'll be all right."

"How do you know?"

He gave her a squeeze. "He's a fighter."

As the paramedics rolled the stretcher out of the house toward the ambulance, James nudged her forward. "Go with them. I'll stay here with the investigators to look for clues."

Lily felt tears slide down her cheeks, unable to process what she'd witnessed. Her brother had been brutally attacked in their home. Someone had tried but failed to kill him. Unbelievable. But James was right. She would go to the hospital to make sure he was all right.

She stepped up into the back of the ambulance and watched the paramedic apply more dressings to the wounds, hang more fluids, and slip an oxygen mask over her brother's mouth and nose.

"I'm Eric," he said when he finally got a minute.

"I'm Lily. Thank you for helping him."

"That's what I'm here for. He's awake and holding on. They'll take good care of him at the hospital."

"I hope so." She had few words for this moment. Everything felt out of control and unknown to her. She'd have to be strong and trust that Zachary would pull through.

Not too long passed before the ambulance roared, lights and sirens, into the Emergency Room entrance. She hopped out and followed the stretcher with her brother into an area marked Triage.

A woman dressed in blue scrubs and holding a clipboard stopped Lily. "Ma'am, you can't go through there. Are you family?"

"Yes, I'm his sister."

"You'll need to get him registered first and then wait in the lounge right over there until he's stabilized."

"Will someone come tell me how he's doing?"

"Yes, I'm Jamie, one of the nurses here in the trauma unit. The doctors will see him. As soon as they're done, they'll be out to speak with you."

"All right, please let me know how he's doing as soon as possible."

"I promise. The lounge is down the hall and to your right." Jamie went back to her station while Lily slowly walked down the corridor.

After she signed a bunch of papers—barely reading them—she found the lounge and melted into one of the chairs. Questions tumbled over and over in her mind. Who had tried to kill her brother?

Could it be a random burglary? Doubtful. Who would burglarize a funeral home?

Had Zachary gotten himself involved in something illegal? More than likely.

She hadn't stayed inside the funeral home long enough to see if anything was missing or if the attacker had left something behind. Surely James would be able to figure that part of things out.

Guilt pushed down on her entire being. Was it somehow tied to her? Was she to blame? What if the killer was retaliating for what happened to Tina?

If so, this attack would be all her fault.

"Hey, I came as soon as I heard." Shanna rushed into the waiting room and took Lily into her arms. "James called Abrams, so we headed over there. Donnie stayed behind at the crime scene. Have you heard anything about Zachary yet? Will he be all right?"

Lily felt spent. Her cheeks were coated with residual tears. "They haven't told me anything yet. The nurse said they'd let us know as soon as they heard."

"What happened?"

"I don't know. Everything looked normal until I opened the front door. He was lying there." Lily brought her hands to her face. "Almost dead."

Then she lost it. Anguish rushed over her body like a demon. Having no control anymore, she let it happen. Shanna lowered her to a chair and, keeping her arm around Lily's shoulder, joined her sister in letting the tears fall. "It's going to be all right. He's going to be fine."

"What if it's not?" Lily wailed. "What if it's all my fault?"

"Why would it be? What have you done?"

"I don't know. What if there's someone still after me? And when they couldn't get me, they went for Zachary?"

"There's no proof of that. Let's just make sure he's okay first, then we'll worry about who did it. I'm sure James and Abrams are busy trying to figure out what happened. They'll figure it out. We need to be strong here for Zachary."

Shanna was right. She had to stop worrying about things she couldn't control. But she was sure of one thing. She would find out who did this to her brother if it was the last thing she did. "Hasn't he been through enough? He was a little kid when Mom and Dad died. That does something to a person."

"We all went through it. You were young too, but you chose not to be a troublemaker."

"I know you say that because as the eldest you had to take us on as a parent. At least I had more time with them that I actually remember. He didn't get that."

"You're saying this out of guilt. But Lily—"

Shanna stared into Lily's eyes. "—this is not your fault. Whoever is doing this is seeking something more than you. We are all in this together. And it doesn't excuse the years of criminal behavior Zachary got himself into. This could be related to that. He might have pissed off the wrong people this time."

"Shanna, that's mean."

"I'm not saying he deserved this, but I don't want you blaming yourself either."

Lily always admired Shanna's strength. Her sister had had no choice but to be strong while taking on two younger siblings. Lily didn't want to argue, but she didn't agree. In her bones, she knew this incident was tied to her, and the guilt would consume her until the killer was caught.

"We need to worry about one thing at a time—Zachary's recovery," Lily added.

"Agreed."

But the time passed slowly—like snail's pace slowly. Between Lily's handwringing and Shanna's incessant knee-bouncing, neither handled the wait well.

"I'm going to find Nurse Jamie," she finally announced to Shanna.

Getting up, she walked down the corridor. She saw a man in scrubs having a conversation with Nurse Jamie. Since this looked promising, Lily approached them. And she decided not to wait for an invitation. "Hi, I'm Lily Reynolds. Any news about my brother, Zachary?"

"Ms. Reynolds, I'm Dr. Miller." He put out his hand while Jamie turned and walked back to her station.

Lily shook his hand. He had rough, wrinkly skin

and gray hair concentrated at the temples. But his eyes had a tenderness to them. He'd probably seen a lot—things she would not care to even think about even though she did spend most of her time with the dead.

"Zachary sustained multiple stab wounds to his torso," Miller said. "We were able to control the bleeding and repair any damage to organs."

The breath she'd been holding poured out all at once.

"It's still too early to say definitively, but he has been stabilized and has been moved to the critical care unit."

"Thank you, Doctor. I'm eternally grateful for all that you and your team have done. Will he be all right?"

"He's hanging in there."

****

Abrams stared down at the crime scene. "There's a lot of blood."

James inhaled much-needed air. He felt like he'd been holding it in since Lily left in the ambulance. "What a disaster."

"I bet that kid has his fair share of enemies. Vandalizing Innovations Funeral Home probably wasn't his first rodeo. He's most likely wrapped up in drugs or every other damn thing."

"Possible," James agreed. "I know he's got a history, but whoever did this didn't have a lot of experience. An expert wouldn't bother with stabbing. It takes too long, and it's messy. Hardly drug-gang action."

"We have to question his girlfriend," Abrams decided. "She'll know what he's been up to better than anyone."

"She's here. And real upset, of course. They've been trying to keep her off the crime scene for the past half hour. I'll go talk to her."

James walked out of the house and toward the patrol cars parked at the entrance. Julie, Zachary's girlfriend, huddled behind the yellow barricade tape. She looked stressed and worried, with her arms crossed over her pale-blue sweater. Strands of straight brown hair blew across her face.

"Julie Horner?"

Her arms tightened. "Yes, tell me he's all right."

"I'm Detective James Rivers. Someone we have not yet identified attacked Zachary tonight. He was taken to Manorview Memorial Hospital."

"Have you heard anything?" she pressed.

"Not yet. His sister Lily is there now."

"I need to go see him."

"You can, but before you go, I wanted to ask you some questions about Zachary."

Her eyes rolled in frustration.

"It won't take long. Do you know anyone who might want to cause him harm? Does he have enemies that you know of? Maybe he owes someone money? Anything you know would help us out."

"He meets a lot of people. He goes out all the time. He never mentioned having problems with anyone in particular. He seems pretty happy with his job, although he talks about wanting to move up in job responsibilities. He knows Lily and Shanna don't trust him enough to give more, but he's been saying that he's ready to take on more if they'd let him. He's had a pretty good track record lately. The only time he went crazy was when he spray-painted that funeral home—

oh crap!" She slapped both hands over her mouth.

"It's fine. I'm not going to charge him for that."

"That was the only time recently that I've seen him really upset—understandable. That crazy woman, going after his family like that. He was trying to protect his family." Tears began to pour down her cheeks. She frantically wiped them away. "Sorry."

"That's okay. I know it's a difficult time. You mentioned he goes out a lot. Where does he go?"

"There's not too much selection around here." She sniffed a couple of times, brushed hair from her face. "He goes to Old Town Bar a lot. They know him pretty well over there."

"Thank you, Julie. Do you need someone to take you to the hospital to see him?"

"No, I'm fine. I can go?"

"Yes."

James watched Julie walk toward her car, sniffling the entire way. This was the worst part of the job. It wasn't dealing with the most horrible criminals you could ever meet or the long hours, sometimes extending way past your ability to have clear judgment. It was dealing with the fallout of the victims's families. The wretched sadness after you've told a mother her child was gone, or a wife her husband wasn't coming home. It was those moments that made him want to quit.

"Was that the girlfriend?" Abrams asked as he walked up to James.

"Yes." James shook himself out of his funk.

"Anything interesting?"

"For the most part, no. She could be lying, but I didn't get that sense. Apparently, Zachary spends his free time at Old Town Bar. That place is the dumping ground for deviants. There's got to be someone there who knows something. I'll check it out."

"Someone there is bound to talk." Abrams held up bagged evidence in one hand. "Meantime, while you were talking to his girlfriend, our guys found this."

"What is it?"

"A scalpel."

"That's the weapon used for the assault?"

"It very well could be by the looks of it." Blood dripped from the sides of the blade, pooling into the corners of the plastic bag.

"I've never seen anyone kill with a scalpel. It's too small, awkward—"

"But sharp."

"This seems more like a last-minute murder. The killer grabbed what he could find in the funeral home. I can't believe someone brought a scalpel here."

"Unless they work around scalpels all day and feel comfortable handling them."

"So a surgeon or someone with a collection of scalpels?"

"Maybe."

James shook his head. "Doesn't feel right."

"It rarely does."

"So far, nothing is missing from the scene. Zachary's wallet was still in his pocket when he was found. None of the closets or drawers were disturbed in the entire funeral home. The hearse is still there. I even checked Lily's room to see if any of her jewelry was gone. Nothing was disturbed. It just doesn't look like a burglary."

"Then we'll have to look for his enemies."

"Or the enemies of the entire family. If the killer

was just targeting Zachary, why would they come here to the funeral home? Why not go to his apartment?"

"True. But maybe they knew he would be here somehow. It's all speculation."

"I can't shake my gut feeling that this is bigger than Zachary."

"Good. That's what I like to hear. This time we will follow your gut."

Chapter Twelve

"You were always a scrappy kid," Lily told Zachary as she sat beside his hospital bed. "But what choice did you have—alone without parents at a young age? It doesn't surprise me you would fight this hard for your life."

His eyes fluttered, and his lips moved. He was in there, listening to her, and it was only a matter of time before he woke up and named who tried to kill him. Julie slept in the lounge chair across from the bed. They had both chosen to stay with Zachary the past two nights. Shanna had gone back to deal with the business while Lily promised to give her updates on his progress and, of course, let her know as soon as he woke up.

Exhausted from the lack of sleep, Lily wracked her brain all night, searching for the culprit. She wouldn't accept the idea that Zachary's attack had been a random act. True, he didn't have the best track record, but none of it was violent. Could it be drug-related retaliation? Had he been involved in a drug ring all this time, and she had no idea? Lily shook her head. *Impossible*.

As the middle child, Lily had grown up struggling to find her own identity alongside a straight-edged older sister and a wild, reckless little brother. But she loved them both. Zachary was not on drugs and, furthermore, not involved in a drug ring. His crimes were considered minor, and he never inflicted actual harm on anyone.

Nope. There had to be another explanation.

"Sixteen stab wounds. That's what the doctor told me. He said you barely made it. You are extremely lucky to be alive. But I knew you'd make it. You always pull through the tough times in your own slightly destructive and sometimes annoying way. I had faith, even though often I tell you you've screwed things up. I know things haven't been easy for you, but you're my little brother, and I love you."

Zachary's eyes flew open.

Lily leaned over him to make sure he could see her. "Zach? Can you hear me?"

Brow furrowed, his gaze moved around the room. He seemed confused and disoriented. He swallowed and grimaced in pain. "Hey."

Lily's heart soared. "Julie! He's awake!"

Julie woke up and scrambled to her feet. She rushed over to his opposite side. "Zachary! Oh, thank God." She put her hand on his chest.

His eyes darted between Lily and Julie a couple of times, then he smiled. "How long have I been out?"

"Two days," Lily said. "How do you feel?"

"A little rough." He raised his arms up, where multiple lines of IV tubing connected to bags of various liquids. "What are these tubes for?"

"They help keep you alive," Julie replied, tears welling up in her eyes.

Lily pulled her phone out, frantically texting Shanna the news. She wanted their sister to know, but she also wanted to pick his memory for clues. "Do you remember anything of what happened?"

Zachary looked at her. He let out a sigh. "I remember going to answer the door, but it was dark out.

I didn't recognize the person at the door. He wore head-to-toe black. Even his face was covered. The last thing I remember is the person rushing at me and tackling me to the ground."

"Do you have any idea who it was?"

"No. The ski mask made it impossible."

"Was he tall, short, thin, fat?" Lily prodded.

"Uh, he was about the same height as me. He wasn't especially large or muscular. Kinda regular."

Lily's heart sank. She'd been waiting for Zachary to not only wake up but also tell her who had attacked him. She hadn't expected Zachary to have problems remembering or that the killer would be impossible to recognize. She had truly believed his memory was the key to this case. Now they had nothing.

"Did he say anything to you? Did he have an accent?"

Zachary grimaced again. "Nothing. He just threw his whole body on top of me. I felt pain in my chest, but I must've passed out soon after."

"Take it easy, Zach," Julie cut in. "Lily, I think he's had enough." Lily backed off and let Julie comfort him. She was being tough on him, but the idea that the attacker roamed free made her crazy. She watched Julie pat his chest and reassure him that everything was going to be all right.

But was it going to be all right?

Julie had been good for Zach. He went from going out every night raising all kinds of hell, then coming to work every other day—if that—to staying home most nights and getting to work early. She'd been the rock he needed to get his head straight. Lily appreciated that.

But Julie was naive and innocent. Their problems

had just begun. Even if Zachary came out of the hospital in one piece, he had a long recovery ahead of them. And with the attacker still at large, who could sleep at night?

"It's all right, Zach. You recover. That's all we want from you," Lily told him with a guarded smile. "We'll take care of the rest." She meant it. With or without Zachary's help, she would find out who attacked him if it was the last thing she did.

Shanna flew into the room fifteen minutes after Lily sent the text.

"He's awake?" She moved to his bedside, leaning over him slightly. "Zachary?"

"Yeah, I guess I'm awake."

She grabbed his hand. "I'm so happy. You've gotten yourself in trouble before, but nothing like this."

"Nope." He shifted his body slowly. "Nothing like this."

"You got lucky this time. But Zachary, I would say you used up eight of your nine lives."

"I agree," he said in a half-slur as his eyes drooped. "That was a close one."

Julie announced, "I think he needs to rest."

"You're probably right. I'm glad I was able to see him awake and talking." Shanna yawned so wide her jaw cracked. "Maybe now I'll get some sleep tonight."

"Even better if he remembered what happened," Lily added.

"He doesn't remember?"

"Nope."

"Not even a shoddy description?"

"Not a thing."

Shanna sighed. "I'm no detective, but that makes

things more challenging."

"It sure does."

From the bed, a deep voice said, "You know I can hear you guys talking about me."

"Sorry, Zach. We love you," Shanna said.

"Yes, don't worry about a thing," Lily added. "We love you."

But as the two sisters walked toward the elevator, leaving Julie at his bedside, Lily's shoulders sagged with the weight of the world and more questions than answers.

****

The following day James stared at the evidence bag on his desk. *A scalpel?* Who would use a scalpel to stab a person? Some random surgeon with a psychotic episode? A disgruntled hospital worker? And how was this connected to Zachary? Was he selling drugs to someone connected to the healthcare field?

Having the scalpel didn't help. In fact, James was more confused than ever. He thought it odd the attack happened at the Reynolds place. Zachary didn't live there. Why had the attacker waited until he was at the funeral home? Had he followed Zachary there? Had he wanted the body to be found by the family for dramatic effect? Or to relay a message?

Maybe the attacker wasn't done yet. Maybe he was waiting for all of the Reynolds to be home. A chill went up his spine. James's mind wandered into the darkest places. He hoped his theory was wrong. The last thing he needed was another threat on Lily's life. It would be more than he could handle.

A text message jolted him out of his thoughts.

–Zach is awake. Come as soon as possible—

James flew to the hospital. He wanted to get there before anyone else started questioning him and possibly confounding his memory. But as he ran down the hospital halls toward the critical care unit, a nurse stopped him in his tracks. He flashed his badge. "Now, Detective. You know he's a very sick young man. We can't have him overwhelmed by visitors."

"I'm trying to find out who did this to him. Please don't stand in the way of getting him justice."

She hesitated.

James knew he was asking her to go against doctor's orders, but this was far too important. He'd pay the price if he had to.

"All right, but you've got five minutes, and then he should rest—"

"Thank you." James rushed past her before she changed her mind.

As soon as he stepped into Zachary's room, Lily embraced him. She'd returned early in the morning to be by her brother's side. She squeezed James tighter than ever before. She needed him.

"He woke up not too long ago," she said, pulling out of his arms. "I'm so relieved. I thought maybe he was going to stay in a semi-awake state forever."

"He's lucky," James said. "I've seen a lot of stabbings, and most people don't pull through."

"He doesn't remember much, though. I don't blame him for blocking it out."

"Does he remember anything?"

"Nothing that helped identify the attacker."

"The nurse is about to kick me out," James said. "Let me ask him some questions alone."

Lily hesitated for a minute. Then she walked over

to Julie. "Let's give James a minute with Zachary. Maybe he can get something out of him."

"All right. It's worth a try." Julie got up and walked out of the room with Lily, leaving the men alone.

James stood at Zachary's bedside. Numerous lines connected him to beeping monitors and IV poles—a sad sight for a young man. But he was awake. That's what mattered the most. "How are you feeling?"

"Wonderful," Zachary moaned. He picked up a bulb-shaped gizmo which James knew from experience would activate the morphine drip. "Couldn't be better."

"You're lucky. Rarely does a case like this one go well. The perpetrator used a scalpel. People use all kinds of things to stab their victims, but I've never seen it happen with a surgical instrument."

"Lucky me." His fist worked the bulb again. "What are you saying—that some doctor stabbed me?"

"I was hoping you would tell me."

"That sucks, 'cause you're out of luck. I don't remember anything."

"You don't remember—or you didn't see anything?"

"I didn't see anything at first, then at some point I must've passed out."

"What did you see before you passed out?"

"Nothing. A guy in all black and a ski mask covering his entire face. He lunged at me and then stabbed me. That's it. I can't identify the guy unless you've got shadows in a lineup." Zachary pushed the pain pump a third time and swore.

James paused to let disappointment settle in. Solving a case without identification from the victim made things more difficult. Sure, they would be looking for DNA evidence, but that would take time, and they might not find anything.

"Do you know if there's someone out there who might be looking for revenge? Have you gotten involved in any drug-related activity?"

Zachary struggled to take in a deep breath. "Man, is that what everyone thinks of me? I don't do drugs."

"No, but the rap sheet from your younger years isn't short." James pulled out a list from his pocket. "Let's see, in one year, you racked up a grand theft auto, trespassing, and arson. You didn't spend much time in jail, but it's not a glowing résumé."

"You don't see anything on there that says drugs, do you?"

"No."

"There's your answer."

"Touché." James folded the sheet back up. "What were you doing at the funeral home at that time of night? You have your own apartment in town, right?"

"Yeah, but Lily had been complaining all week about unloading the new caskets and taking them up to the showroom. I thought I would stop in and get that done before the next morning. You don't want Lily mad at you. It's not a pretty sight."

James smiled. He had no doubt about her she-wolf tendencies, but he didn't mind. In fact, he liked it.

"All right, Detective. I heard you were in here." A nurse stood at the doorway with her arms crossed and a raised eyebrow like she meant business. "You've had more than enough time with him. He needs his rest—doctor's orders."

"That's fine with me. I'm done here."

James went back out into the hallway and found Julie and Lily standing by a window. "He has a long recovery ahead. He's lucky to have you, Julie."

"I'll take good care of him while you find out who did this to him," she said.

"I'll do the best I can."

She gave him a quick smile and walked back into Zachary's room.

"I missed you," James said, stepping closer to Lily. With all the recent drama, he'd almost forgotten to appreciate her beauty. He knew she'd been sleeping in Zachary's hospital room for the past two nights, but even so, her skin glowed and her eyes sparkled with determination. He looked at her as equal parts soldier and angel. "Zachary's awake. Tina is locked away. Things are looking up."

"His attacker is on the loose. Probably waiting until one of us is alone."

"Then I won't leave you alone."

"You can't be with me all the time."

"I can sure try."

"Even so, we need a plan."

James took in a breath. "Why can't we take a moment to appreciate being together instead of jumping into the next pile of danger?"

"Take a moment? All right. How would you like to do that?"

James stepped even closer to her until his mouth brushed her ear. "I really missed you." Then he kissed her ear. "Don't worry. I'm not going to let anything happen to you."

She turned her head to face him. "I know, but I'm not sure what you want will matter to the attacker."

"It matters. Right now, it's the only thing that matters to me."

Lily smiled. "I missed you, too."

His arms went around her. "We're on the same team. I promise I will find out who did this."

"I know we will."

He pulled out of their embrace. "We?"

She threw her arms around him again. "Yes, we."

Chapter Thirteen

Yikes.

Lily lifted a box of embalming fluid, carrying it from the delivery entrance in the back to the embalming room. Zachary had been discharged a few days ago and was home in his apartment—healing up—with Julie on standby. With him out of commission, she'd be doing a lot of the heavy lifting around the funeral home.

She groaned and panted all the way to the embalming room, dropping the box on the floor. After a couple of seconds of rest, she began stacking each bottle onto the shelves with a hard push. Her frustration with how slowly the case had progressed made her day job difficult.

Not one lead. How could that be? She pushed the last bottle onto the shelf and slammed the cabinet door shut. What was James doing? Lily understood his reluctance to involve her in the case. The victim was her brother, but James would be reluctant no matter who was involved. She felt powerless and useless. Not something she was used to.

Lily's stomach grumbled. Saturday morning, and she had not had breakfast yet. She walked toward the kitchen. Coffee and scones should fix things, she hoped.

"Good morning," Shanna said, barely looking up as Lily poured herself some coffee.

Lily sank onto one of the island bar stools, eyeing the decadent pile of blueberry scones from Sweet Teeth Bakery. "Is it a good morning?"

"In other grumpy news, I heard something interesting at the bakery this morning."

Lily didn't have the energy to ask. Her brother's near-death experience had been plenty for her to deal with.

Shanna took a sip of coffee, carefully placed the mug back down on the island. Her face scrunched up as she did. "I heard Innovations Funeral Home is back up and running."

Lily stared at her.

"Chris Tuchman is their new leader. I don't really know what that means for us."

Lily bit off a sugary corner of the largest scone and waited until the sweet goodness slid down her throat before answering. "Is this going to be an issue for us? Is he a real threat?"

"I can't imagine why he'd be anything other than a business threat. Even that's questionable given how poorly the business was doing before."

"Tina was a smart businesswoman, but she let her personal problems get in the way and affect her ability to make sound decisions. I've got to hand it to Chris. I would not want to take on a business whose previous owner is in jail for attempted murder. Seems like a mountain to climb in terms of public redemption."

"I agree. I don't think Innovations will be a real threat to us," Shanna said after another sip. Then she made the same disgusted face after the first sip. "This coffee tastes terrible."

Lily eyed the mug. "How old are these beans?"

Shanna dumped the rest of her coffee into the sink. "I don't know but stay away from this batch."

"Did you hear from Zachary?"

"I talked to him this morning. He sounds better. How's the investigation going? Have the three musketeers figured it all out yet?"

"Three musketeers?"

Shanna coughed. "James, Abrams, and you. Aren't you part of the investigation team now?"

"Sort of. I don't think they've gotten anywhere. Zach couldn't identify the guy, and James hasn't included me on this one that much. I think he's worried about the impact it might have on my emotions, but after I finish up the chores here, I think I'm going to head over there and get more involved."

Shanna bent over and coughed again.

Lily didn't like her color. "Are you all right?"

Her sister cleared her throat but didn't straighten. "Not sure."

Then she coughed so hard she fell over.

Lily leaped off the bar stool and rushed over to Shanna. "Are you choking?"

The coughing stopped, but her breathing was labored. "I'm not choking, but I feel like I can't breathe."

"Should I call an ambulance?"

Struggling to take in air, Shanna grabbed at her throat.

Lily grabbed her phone and dialed 9-1-1 first. Then she called James, who answered on the first ring. "Something's wrong with my sister. You need to get over here." She hung up and checked on Shanna.

Again, Lily felt powerless and vulnerable. She had

no idea what was wrong with her sister. Her eyes were open, and she was conscious, but she gasped and struggled to breathe. Lily helped her to the living room, where she laid her on the couch until the ambulance showed up. Shanna's eyes closed as she fell in and out of consciousness.

Tears tumbled onto Lily's cheeks as she struggled to keep Shanna awake. "Come on, come on. Stay with me, sweetie."

Finally, the ambulance showed up, and the paramedics stormed in with all their equipment. Lily moved aside and let them treat her. James rushed in after the paramedics.

He put his arms around her, drawing her farther from the scene. "What happened?"

Lily hid her face in his chest. She couldn't face another family member being in trouble. "I don't know. It seemed to come out of nowhere. One minute she was fine. The next, she began coughing and then couldn't breathe."

"It's all right. The paramedics will help her. What was she doing right before it happened?"

"We were talking in the kitchen. I was eating a scone, and she was drinking coffee. She was acting normal. Then she couldn't breathe."

"Does she have any food allergies?"

"I don't know. It all happened so fast."

He kissed her on the forehead. "Everything's going to be all right. She's going to be fine. You go in the ambulance with her. I'll stay here to look around, then I'll meet you at the hospital. Abrams should be over here in a minute."

Lily leaned into him a while longer. She wanted

Shanna to be fine but the thought of going to the hospital again, waiting for news all by herself, made her sick to her stomach. Her family was falling apart, one after another.

"This is not a coincidence, James. We're being targeted."

"Maybe. Let's make sure Shanna is all right first. We can talk about it later."

Saying nothing, she reluctantly pulled out of his embrace and followed the paramedics toward the ambulance. This was no coincidence. Someone was targeting her family.

If that was the case, was she next?

****

After Lily left in the ambulance, James moved straight to the kitchen. This was no simple allergic reaction. The Reynolds were being targeted by someone hell-bent on getting rid of the entire family. If that were true, it had to be someone close. Someone who knew them well. Someone who hated them.

As he looked around, nothing looked out of the ordinary in the kitchen. It looked as Lily had described it. Scones were on the table, and hot coffee was still in the pot. Lily said she had the scone, and she was fine. But Shanna drank the coffee. James stared at the pot. He should not take this lightly. He had no idea what was in there. With Shanna coming so close to death, he didn't want to touch it or inhale it. He'd have to wait until the crime scene investigators showed up with their protective gear and tools to take samples.

"Where is she?" Abrams's voice made James jump.

"Geez, a little warning next time would be nice."

Abrams grabbed James's arm like he meant business. "Is Shanna all right?"

"She will be," he replied quickly, but technically he didn't know for sure. "She was having trouble breathing. According to Lily, it all started after she drank the coffee." He pointed toward the machine. "We need to have it checked out."

"You've got to be kidding me. Poison. She's been poisoned?" Abrams rubbed his eyes in disbelief. "Holy crap. Who would do this?"

"I don't know, but I think you should go to the hospital to see her. You're too…invested. I'll deal with the crime scene. There's got to be a connection to Zachary's attempted murder. Someone is trying to off the entire Reynolds family."

Abrams stared at the floor as if trying to process the new development. He ground his jaw like he was channeling all his anger there. "If that's true, you better keep a close eye on Lily."

James glared at Abrams. The last thing he wanted to think about was Lily's attempted murder.

"I'm just saying. Why would they stop here? There's one more Reynolds—"

"All right, I got the message. Go see how Shanna's doing. I'll stay here. We need to find out what's in this coffee and who's responsible."

"Fine. I'm off. Let me know if you find anything. We need to get this jerk." Abrams left without another word while crime scene investigators filed one by one into the kitchen.

James hated himself. He hadn't been very sensitive toward Abrams. If Lily were in the hospital, James would've expected a less callous approach. But he'd been so focused on preserving the crime scene he'd neglected to make sure Abrams was okay. His anger was completely justified. If the roles were reversed, James probably would've been arrested, fired from his job, and beat up all at the same time.

"Anything need to be bagged up?" Demetri asked as he put on latex gloves.

"We need to get this coffee tested for poison."

"Poison?"

"I'd be careful with this. Who knows what's in there. Could be cyanide, strychnine, or ricin. Better gown up just in case."

Demetri walked over to the rest of the team, telling them to clear out, and then he came back over with a large bag. "I brought the suits in that black bag over there. I'm going to clear out the other guys for safety, first."

James helped him pull out the yellow suits. Putting them on was probably overkill, but he had no idea what he was dealing with. James stepped into the yellow suit and pulled the arms on. He stretched the latex gloves over his fingers and then zipped the suit up. Then came the hood with respirators sticking out from the sides. Not how he'd pictured the rest of the day but also not his first chemical scare. The worst case he'd seen was a chemical scare in the middle of Times Square on a hot summer day. Sheer panic had ensued, and crowd control had been a bitch.

Once Demetri put his hood over his dark curls and gave him a thumbs-up, James moved toward the coffee machine. "Should we take the whole thing?"

"I would." Demetri nodded. "You don't want to leave anything behind that may be contaminated."

James unplugged the coffee machine. "Wrap up the whole thing in plastic, then we'll put it in one of those containers."

"Already on it." Demetri took out a large tube of clear wrap from one of the white boxes the team had brought in to collect evidence, and he began wrapping up the coffee machine. "Dang. Haven't had one of these in a long time. You think there will be multiple strikes?"

James thought about Lily, shook his head, and let out a frustrated breath. "There better not be."

Chapter Fourteen

Lily slapped Shanna's test results on James's desk. "The doctors said she was poisoned."

She left the hospital royally pissed. She wanted answers from the one person who should care the most. That is, *if* he cared about her as much as he said he did.

"She could've died, James. Doesn't that bother you? What have you been doing about finding the person responsible?"

He rubbed at his eyes. "I'm working on it. I've been here all night."

"Really? What have you been doing about it?"

James took a deep breath. "I'm waiting on test results from the lab—"

"I just gave you the test results. It says *formaldehyde*. My sister was poisoned with it."

He grabbed the test results from his desk. "That's an odd choice for a poison. I've never seen that before. It's not the first choice people turn to."

"Why?"

"You can get more common poisons in hardware stores. People use them as pesticides. Formaldehyde isn't lying around in homes, and most don't know what it does if ingested."

"It's lying around in my house. We use it for embalming. The would-be killer could've used our own supply to put in Shanna's coffee. That doesn't tell us

154

much about who did it. The bottle has a skull and cross bones on it. Anyone could guess it's poison."

"The attacks on Zachary and then on Shanna seem to be orchestrated. They were planned out. The killer thought about what weapons to use prior to the attacks. If they used items from the house, then it would be an inside job—someone who knows the inside of your house really well. Do you know anyone who fits that description?"

"No." Lily paced the floor, frustration growing with each passing second. Finally, she stopped in front of his desk. "Unless you're once again suggesting that I would try to murder my own family?"

"Of course not. But there's got to be someone you know in the business who might be capable of it."

She sat with a thump in the chair in front of him. Her index finger waved around as she spoke. "You know what I think? I think you're holding out on me. I think you know more about this case but don't want me involved due to your personal issues. I think you're keeping valuable information from me because you don't want to deal with my possibly getting hurt. Is that it?" She stood up.

"No, Lily, stop this. I'm not keeping anything from you." James came out of his chair and walked toward her. He stood in front of her, holding her arms. "Look at me. Listen to what I'm saying. I'm not keeping anything from you. I have no leads. I'm trying really hard. All morning I've been staring at that scalpel, hoping something would come to mind."

"Scalpel? What scalpel?"

"That one." He pointed to the bag next to a pile of folders on his desk.

Lily reached over and lifted the bag up in front of her face. "Is this the weapon used to attack Zachary?"

"Yes."

"And you didn't think I would want to see this? Aren't I part of your team? Didn't we decide that I could help solve cases?"

"Yes…but it's your family."

"See? That's exactly what I mean. You're keeping this from me." She shook the bag in front of his face. "I demand that you stop doing that."

James sighed. "Fine. I can't help it. I can't help but want to protect you. I'm trying. I really am. You want to know what I really think?"

"That would be good."

"I hate this. I hate the thought of you going out there looking for evidence and possibly getting yourself killed. So shoot me!"

Lily wanted to smile, but she didn't want him to know she was flattered by his words. She needed to show her strength and equal partnership. She needed to be clear about how she wanted to be treated if they were going to have any sort of relationship.

"You're going to have to fight that urge. I'm not going anywhere. I want to be part of this case, and you'll just have to get used to it. Besides, who else is going to tell you that scalpels and formaldehyde are routinely used by funeral homes to take care of the recently deceased?"

James looked at her. His eyebrows were pulled up in surprise. "Are you saying the person who did this works in a funeral home?"

"Possibly. Who else would have formaldehyde laying around? And who else uses a scalpel to stab someone? A knife would be more common and probably easier to use than a surgical instrument. This person knows his way around a scalpel and knows the hazards of formaldehyde."

James looked like he was dreading what he'd say next. "There's only one other funeral home in Manorview unless the person came from out of town. But that seems less likely given how it was just your family members who were targeted."

"I'm certain our attacker works at Innovations Funeral Home."

"But who? Tina's behind bars. Is someone acting in her place or on their own?"

"I can't be sure, but Chris Tuchman was pretty loyal to her. Maybe he convinced Simon, their embalmer, to take us out once and for all. It would make their business more successful if ours was gone."

James paused like he was processing all the possibilities. "You can't stay at your place all alone. It's too dangerous."

"I don't want to be a coward either."

"Don't be ridiculous. You can't stay there. If your theory is correct, you're next in line. In fact, you shouldn't go home today."

"Excuse me? I've got clients lined up." Hands raised in frustration, she walked away from him. "I've got a business to run and no one to help right now."

"What's all the commotion?" Abrams poked his head into the office. "I heard you two yelling down the hall, then saw you waving your arms around through the glass in the hallway."

James waved him into the office. After Abrams shut the door, James said, "Lily thinks the killer might be Simon or Chris from Innovations."

"Cook and Tuchman? The guys who worked for Tina? We interviewed her entire staff. They were all clean."

"Shanna was poisoned with formaldehyde, and Zachary was stabbed with a scalpel. Those are embalmer's tools," Lily said. "Plus, Innovations is under new management now. Maybe Chris Tuchman is acting under Tina's orders. Maybe she's not done yet. Maybe her final act is to get rid of my entire family."

Both Abrams and James acknowledged her revelation.

"I think for now you should stay with her," Abrams said, pointing at James. "I'll send some guys up to Innovations to take everyone in for questioning, and we'll need to get a search warrant."

"Thanks, Detective Abrams," Lily said.

James elbowed him. "You're my hero."

"Anytime. Why don't you two take off? It's been a rough couple of days. I want to get all of this orchestrated and then head to the hospital to see Shanna again."

"She was awake when I saw her this morning. She's coming around, thank goodness."

She couldn't help but notice the concern washing over Abrams's face. He loved her.

Lily knew that look. She'd seen it on James's face countless times. "Shanna was very lucky. But I want to go to my place. I feel like I've been living in hospitals lately."

"That's fine. I'm coming with you," James said.

"Probably a good idea," Abrams said. "I'll let you know how it's going at the Innovations place. Don't worry. We'll be fine without you," Towering over James, he leaned in closer. "Whatever you do today, don't let Lily out of your sight."

"I'm not planning on it."

Chapter Fifteen

From her bedroom window, Lily watched the sun slowly disappear behind the trees. She was used to having death around her, but not the kind that took her family members. The attacker was still on the loose, and yet she'd gone back to the scene of both crimes, probably where the attacker could get to her. Stupid? Maybe. But she wanted to meet the person who threatened to annihilate her family.

"I checked all the doors and windows," James said. "Everything's locked up tight. I also have two patrol units stationed nearby."

Lily watched him from the corner of her eye, checking his gun to make sure it was loaded and ready for whatever might come. Her lungs swelled as she took in a deep breath. She enjoyed his attentiveness. It wasn't something she was used to. All her life, she'd had to be strong and logical. She had to admit it was nice to let someone else worry for once.

When he seemed satisfied, James came up behind her. "If this guy thinks he's going to get through me, he's got another thing coming." She felt him sweep her hair aside, leaving the back of her neck exposed. A tingle ran down her spine as she felt his lips brush against the skin of her neck.

"You really think we're safe?"

His arms went around her waist while he continued

to kiss her neck. "I think we're safe for the night."

Sensing a change in him, she turned around. His touch was not simply to comfort her or make her feel protected. This was an entirely different feeling—it was a feeling based on need.

Without hesitation, his lips landed on top of hers. It was a deep, hungry kiss from the start, as if he had limited time to show her how he felt about her. She reciprocated, needing the same thing. A combination of euphoria and desire came galloping out of their bodies and drove them into each other's arms.

A wildfire of energy pushed them toward the bed. A few more passionate kisses and Lily's shirt flew over her head. The frenzy continued. She couldn't get enough of his taut biceps and chest. In her haste, she'd managed to unbutton his shirt and take a peek at the numerous tattoos starting at his biceps and moving down his arms and across his chest. A knight in full armor standing with his sword out, ready to fight, had been tattooed on his chest. She didn't have to ask him to know why he'd picked that tattoo. She knew he carried the burden of being not just her protector but also everyone's knight in shining armor.

She traced the tattoo down his chest with her finger, moving down until his belt stopped her from going any farther. He caught her finger and smiled mischievously. He threw off his weapon harness and shirt while she laid her head on the pillow. Whatever fear or trepidation she had earlier seemed trivial as he nestled his lips against her neck and chest.

Her skin flushed with excitement. The fire in her belly urged her on until she felt like her whole body would burst into flames. Her hands went down the lean muscles of his back—rock solid, but his skin was soft and buttery. He came back up from her chest to her mouth. His tongue diving in with urgency. His hands rubbed down her thighs, squeezing them gently. He pulled at her panty, sliding it off rather smoothly. His hand traced the back of her thigh, making her insides ache. He pushed off his pants, revealing the rest of his ink. The knight's legs wrapped around a black stallion whose strong, elegant features went down his hip and right leg.

"It's beautiful."

"Nothing compared to you."

Lily was ready. She knew in her heart and mind the need they had for each other rivaled what the evening had in store for them. At least, she hoped.

The pitch-black darkness that had fallen over the last several hours made them feel like strangers in the same bed. But her body had never felt more connected to James than it did tonight. Hers lay spent with exhaustion, but her mind sped up in exhilaration. She couldn't help the onslaught of thoughts and ideas she wanted to present to him.

"James? Are you still awake?"

She heard him breathe in deeply. "Barely."

"Do you think we'll be okay?"

"Yeah, I told you the place is secure."

"No, not that. Will we be able to get over our demons and move on?"

"I don't know. You said you don't date cops—sure fooled me."

She smiled. "Does that mean you think you can get over worrying about protecting me?"

"I'm not going to stop worrying about protecting

you, but I might let some things slide."

"I'm serious. Are you going to run away the first moment that I am threatened or hurt?"

"I'm still here, aren't I? And both of those things have happened." Lily felt his fingers lightly caress her arm. "You don't have to worry. We're too similar to stay away from each other. I'm not going anywhere."

Lily wanted to drop it. She didn't want a perfect evening to turn into the complete opposite just because she couldn't let it go.

"I'm going downstairs to get a drink. Want anything?"

A light snore came out in a response.

"Good. Glad my watchdog has finally bit the dust." Lily got up and felt her way toward the bathroom, where she found her bathrobe and slippers. She wandered down to the bottom of the stairs and listened to the silence for a second.

Everything seemed as it should. Quiet. When she felt satisfied, Lily walked toward the embalming room. As soon as she flicked on the lights and walked into the room, a strong chemical odor burned her nose.

That was odd. Her sister was a fanatic about cleaning up after she was finished with clients. But maybe she hadn't had a chance before she was poisoned. Lily rarely spent much time in the embalming room. This was Shanna's territory. Whatever that smell was, she'd come back in the morning to clean it up.

In the meantime, she couldn't resist the urge to do her own investigation into the possible missing scalpel and embalming fluid. Since Zachary's injury, she'd taken over the chore of restocking supplies. She would know if something was missing. But looking at the bottles of embalming fluid lined up one after the other just as she had stocked them told her none were missing.

She moved to the drawer filled with embalming tools. She'd recently ordered new trocars and tubing since those tended to get damaged the fastest, but the number of scalpels never changed. She counted them— six in total. They were all accounted for, which meant only one thing—the killer had brought his own supply. The only other place in town with an abundance of those items was Innovations Funeral Home.

With his in-depth knowledge as an embalmer, the killer had to be Simon Cook.

"Did you figure it out?"

Lily jumped and turned as Simon, cool and calm, walked into the room, shutting the door behind him. Surely, he heard the pounding of her heart against her chest.

"Don't scream. I want your boyfriend to have pleasant dreams and continue to think you're safe."

"How did you get in here?"

"I've been waiting so long for this moment. Your detective was so thorough in locking up the house, he didn't realize he locked me in. I've been here the whole time. Waiting."

Lily barely heard him through the pounding in her ears. She felt lightheaded and tiny, like a gazelle facing a lion.

"I must admit I didn't succeed in killing your brother and sister. The Reynolds family members have proven to be hard to kill, but I will say this, I won't make the same mistake a third time."

"Whatever Tina's paying, I'll give you double."

"She's not paying me, but your very existence is killing Innovations. You may not know this, but I am the best embalmer in town. If you weren't around, everyone would know that, and we would be the most successful funeral home. But unfortunately, people like tradition, so unless I get rid of you, Innovations will never be great." He pumped his fists. "And I want it to be great."

"I could hire you. We could use your talent here. If we join forces, everyone wins—"

"I don't want to join forces with you. I want to conquer Reynolds Funeral Home for good and let someone else take first place, and the only way to do that is to get rid of you. I know your sister and brother will live, but they won't run the business ever again, and the only way to be sure of it is to show them I mean it. Speaking of which, did you notice a smell in here?"

"Yes," Lily whispered. What horrible plans had he come up with? *Torture? Suffocation? Or worse, mutilation?* Horrible things ran through her mind until she thought she might pass out.

"You should recognize the smell. It's something you deal with on a daily basis. More Shanna than you, but still, it shouldn't be foreign to you. Any guesses?"

Lily shook her head. She already knew but didn't want to answer. Her eyes welled up with tears. She was going to die here in the embalming room. Her vision of living a long life and dying of natural causes surrounded by family went up in smoke.

"I doused the room with embalming fluid before you came in," Simon admitted, almost bragging. "I could go on and on about the miracle that is formaldehyde. It has the ability to preserve and disinfect but is also highly flammable. Convenient." He pulled out a matchbox from his back pocket. "Any last words?"

The door smashed against the wall. James stood there, pointing his weapon at Simon. "I'll shoot you before you can strike that match."

"Is that you, Detective Rivers? Here to show your girlfriend you really can solve crimes? I don't really think that's fair, though. I came to you. You didn't even need to come and find me. I did all the work, really."

"Your tirade is over, Simon. It's time to pay for all the damage you've done."

"I heard something the other day about you. You know how small-town gossip goes. I heard from Zachary that you let a past girlfriend die in your arms. Can't imagine that felt too good. A cop whose job is to serve and protect couldn't even save his own woman. Pretty pathetic if you ask me."

"I'm here now," James taunted. "Ready to shoot you if you prefer."

Lily watched Simon fiddle with the matchbox. He seemed to be thinking through his options. She didn't know where this was going, but he clearly didn't want to give up. When he opened the matchbox, she didn't hesitate. "Shoot him."

Simon gaped at her. "What?"

"Shoot him, James. He's not going with you."

"She has a strong voice, James. She might be too tough for you," Simon said as he struck a match and flame shot up.

"Shoot him!"

Before another second went by, James pulled the trigger and kept on pulling until Simon crumbled to the ground. He let go of the lit match and fell on top of it, effectively snuffing out the flame.

All the air Lily had been holding in came flooding out. Close, very close to complete incineration. She looked at James. The hand holding the gun trembled. He stared down at Simon, making sure he didn't move. Lily knew this would be hard for him.

"It's okay. Everything's okay. He's dead. I'm safe. Everyone is safe."

He looked at her, finally lowering the hand with the gun. He took in a breath as tears welled in his eyes.

Lily ran to him. He squeezed her tight—too tight. But she understood. The exact scenario he had wanted to avoid had played out and, thankfully, it had gone in the right direction.

"Are you all right?"

"I'm fine. He was going to blow up the place. He doused the room with embalming fluid."

James shook his head. "Crazy. All for what?"

"Glory. A way to legitimize himself."

"This went our way this time, but—"

"I know what you're going to say. I think it's more of an example of how different this situation is than a warning for the future. Don't get me wrong, your job is dangerous, and that's hard on me, but our pasts shouldn't stop us from moving on."

James smiled, and she had a feeling that was the most she was going to get.

"I'm calling Abrams. We'll need to get the scene preserved as evidence."

"Makes sense. It's gonna be a long night."

"We can stay at my place while Abrams babysits the crime scene investigators." James put his phone to his ear, walking away from the embalming room.

Lily stared at the gruesome scene. Blood had fanned out around Simon as he lay face down on the floor. James had fired at least three or four shots, making sure he hit his target. She had a knack for solving crimes, but could she shoot anyone? A chill went down her spine at the memory of hearing gunshots thundering throughout her childhood home the evening her parents were savagely murdered. Nope. She wasn't sure she could ever shoot a gun. Did that make her weak? Or a poor excuse for a pseudo-detective? A loud sigh escaped her lips.

James walked back in. "What's wrong?"

"Nothing. I was thinking about how difficult this is for me."

He waited in silence for her to go on.

"You might be right. I'm not cut out for this."

"I never said—"

"It hits too close to home. I tried to ignore it, but I'm just as messed up as you are. This is probably how it was for my parents." Tears welled, clouding her vision.

"Oh, Lily." James opened his arms for her to go to him. "It's not the same thing."

She went to him without hesitation. His embrace comforted her. She knew he wouldn't judge her moment of weakness or make any conclusions about her abilities, and that's how she knew he loved her.

"Stinks in here. Don't you guys smell that?" Abrams asked as he walked in with a gun in his hand but held to his side.

"Embalming fluid. Simon was going to blow the place up to get rid of the last of the Reynolds family. I shot him instead."

Abrams got closer to Simon's facedown body. "Good work. The matchbox is right next to him."

"He had a flame in his hand, but he landed on top of it and blew it out."

"He blew out his own flame?"

"Yup."

"I wouldn't have guessed Simon Cook for the bad guy, but it makes sense." Abrams shrugged his shoulders. "There's got to be a link to Tina."

"I would agree. She'll talk for a lesser sentence. They all do. Tom Bleyer gave us Sarah Taylor, and Tina will tell us if she's got anything else up her sleeve. It's time for Innovations Funeral Home to be shut down for good."

"Agreed. Good riddance. I'm going to tell the guys to start securing the scene." Abrams nodded his head toward them and left the room to wait for the investigators.

"Are you all right?" James asked.

Lily sucked in a breath. "Yes, I'll be fine."

"I want you to know you don't have to prove anything to me. I know you're a good detective, and if your past makes this difficult for you, that's fine and understandable. You are no less of a detective."

She smiled, already knowing he would feel that way. "I hope you're right."

"I know I am." He grabbed her hand. "Come on, let's go. We'll forget about this place tonight."

"Sounds like a plan."

Chapter Sixteen

Shanna was discharged from the hospital three days after Lily's standoff with Simon Cook. Innovations Funeral Home was shut down, leaving Marcia and Chris out of work. Marcia easily slid into helping Lily with her workload and expressed her thanks to even have a job. Chris Tuchman, on the other hand, was another issue.

Sitting opposite him in their office, Shanna and Lily tried to understand how he would fit into the Reynolds business.

"I'm highly organized and can take an enormous amount of pressure. At Innovations, I was used to a constantly changing playing field. I think having someone around to keep things organized and to troubleshoot is hugely valuable."

Lily looked at Shanna. She'd recovered enough from the poisoning to resume work at the funeral home, but her eyes had lost some sparkle. Having more help here would probably do her some good.

She turned back to Chris. "We've never had anyone work here as a manager. Usually, we have group meetings and discuss any issues among ourselves. Plus, after what happened with Tina, how can we trust you?"

"I never knew what she was up to. I knew she wanted her business to succeed, but I never knew the extent of her plans. My job was to come up with strategies to help the business. That's it." His right knee bounced up and down.

"Can we trust you?" Shanna asked. "Seems like nothing good comes out of Innovations. Marcia's too innocent to worry about, but Tina confided in you. You had to have known what she was up to."

Chris shook his head. "I did not know."

"And what about Simon? There had to be something about him that stuck out to you. You were his manager."

"I knew Tina was using him to spy on your business. He would go out to bars with Zachary to find out bits of information."

"What type of information?"

"Mostly about what everyone was up to. Zachary talked about you and James starting up a romance. That sort of thing. Simon was passionate about his work. He came in every day and did his embalming with pride. He wasn't a troublemaker or difficult to deal with. There were no red flags. He knew embalming inside and out—that was good enough for us."

Shanna continued. "Did you sense a special relationship between him and Tina? Maybe something closer than you would expect from an employee and their boss?"

"I did not know they had been making any sort of plans for Simon to carry forward her ideas. Like I said, he was spying on you through Zachary, but the extent to which she had gone was way beyond anything I ever imagined."

"How about when you called the cops, accusing me of trying to break into Innovations?" Lily asked.

Chris's lips twitched.

At this point, it was probably obvious to everyone that she *was* trying to break into Innovations, but she wanted to see how he would handle her question.

"I was doing my job, which was to protect the best interest of Innovations. I'm sorry the cops got involved, but I feel I was doing the right thing at that time—before we knew what Tina was all about. I would do the same for Reynolds Funeral Home."

Lily liked his answer. She detected no intent to mislead them. Zachary, who held a legitimate partnership position in their business, had been completely against hiring anyone who previously worked at Innovations. She didn't blame him, but why punish everyone associated with Tina? Lily considered herself a good judge of character. She really saw no reason not to hire Chris.

"Would you like to work here?"

"Yes, very much."

Lily looked at Shanna, who smiled in her usual gracious way.

"I guess you're hired, Chris. Welcome to Reynolds Funeral Home."

Chris smiled and shook their hands. "Thank you. I promise you won't regret it."

"I'm sure we won't. Can you start tomorrow?"

"Yes. I'd love to."

"Great. Shanna will show you out. See you tomorrow, Chris."

"Bye, Lily, and thank you."

Lily leaned back in her office chair. She hoped she was making the right choice. Bringing the enemy into her home was either going to ruin them, or it was a step toward converting Marcia and Chris into decent people. You know what they say, keep your friends close, keep your enemies closer.

"Knock, knock." James stood in the doorway of her office. "Was that Chris Tuchman I saw on the way out? What did you break into now?"

He had the gleeful look of a naughty toddler, making it all the more difficult for her to be upset.

"Very funny. We just hired him."

The playful expression on James's face vanished. "You can't be serious."

"We never play games at the Reynolds Funeral Home."

"Worst idea ever. This means I'm going to have to pay even closer attention to this place."

"No need, Detective. We are self-sufficient."

"I think you like getting into trouble. In fact, I think you like the challenge."

Lily grinned. "Is that right?"

"That's right. I think you like it so much you're going to love the case I need you to help me with."

Lily's interest sparked. "Tell me."

"We found a body by the footpath near Black River. The victim was identified as Samantha Riley, a female in her twenties. We think she was jogging along the river when she was attacked. The marks on her neck suggest she was strangled."

"That's horrible. I haven't heard of that kind of crime in Manorview."

"Abrams has talked about a few similar cases that happened years ago. But nothing lately."

"How can I help?"

"You've seen quite a few bodies in your line of

work. I want you to take a look at her. She has a tattoo on her back. I want to know if you've ever seen it before on anyone else you've…handled here."

"Usually, I cover up strange marks. That's my job. And I don't ask any questions about them. That's usually none of my business."

"I understand, but for now, you have to take off your mortician's cap and replace it with a detective's cap. If you've seen these marks on other bodies, I want to know about it. Usually, when a symbol is left on a body, the killer does it on purpose to let everyone know he was the one who did it. It's like they are branding each victim."

"Is it a single tattoo?"

"Appears so."

"That's all you need me to do? I can interview suspects or break into a house if you need me."

James grinned. "I don't think that will be necessary. We don't have any suspects, but I'll be sure to keep you in mind if I need a B and E man."

"With Marcia here to help, I have more free time to help catch killers."

James sighed. "There's nothing about what you just said that makes me happy."

"You'll get used to it. I promise after the first case working together, you'll wish we had done it sooner."

"I somehow doubt that."

"I'm free now. Shall I go with you to view the body?"

"Do I have a choice?"

"No."

Chapter Seventeen

"Show me," Lily said.

Surrounded by the clinical white walls of Manorview's hospital morgue, the medical examiner, Dr. Paul Elliot, and James stood at either side of a gurney, staring down at the victim's body. The smell of death and chemicals burned her nostrils. The average person would find this scene repellent but not Lily. The familiarity and comfort level she had with death made anyone else's skin crawl.

"The tattoo marking is here," Dr. Elliot said, propping up the left shoulder with a gloved hand. "I'm not a tattoo artist, but it looks like the person who did it had some skills. And the wound has had a chance to heal, so it wasn't done postmortem."

The hairs on Lily's arms stood up. "I have seen this tattoo before. At the time, I didn't think much of it. It looked like a bad tattoo, and since the family members don't usually see the client's back during the viewing, I didn't cover it up with makeup."

"Does that mean you've seen them in other places besides the person's back?" James asked.

"I've seen them on the upper arms and upper chest areas."

"All female?"

She thought for a moment before responding. "Now that you mention it, yes."

He cocked one eyebrow. "You know what that means, right?"

She shrugged. "Whoever is doing this is targeting females."

"Yes, but it also means we might have a serial killer on our hands."

Lily sucked in a breath. "Then there could be a bunch more." She shook her head in dismay. "What do you make of the symbol?"

"A lightning bolt with a stake through it," James replied. "Seems like a typical gang symbol which might explain why the tattoo passed for professional. Some gang members ink tats on each other all the time."

"A gang?" Her voice raised in a squeak. "Here in Manorview?"

"They're everywhere, Lily. You'd be surprised. That type doesn't care for the rules or law enforcement. Sometimes, they don't really care if they die either—makes my job harder." He pointed at Samantha's tattoo. "How many of these symbols have you seen? And did they all look the same?"

"I would say I've seen four or five, and the symbols were about the same. I thought since they appeared on mostly younger females that this was a social trend of some sort, like a fad or something. A lot of them have piercings too, but I never thought much about that either."

"Did the same females with the symbols also have piercings?"

"I think so."

"The killer had a type. Do you happen to recall or have knowledge of the cause of death of those women?"

"We usually do know the cause of death. It helps us decide if we need to do anything special to the body for presentation. Is Samantha's death consistent with strangulation, Dr. Elliot?"

"Yes, as you can see here." He pointed to the neck area on the corpse. "Redness and bruising suggest she died from strangulation. There were no other injuries found on the body."

Lily noted the blank look on Dr. Elliot's face as he discussed the findings. His dry demeanor matched his official-looking white coat. It didn't stop the shivers running along her spine as he bluntly described how Samantha died. Lily was used to covering up the victim's problems and portraying a peaceful image to the family. Discussing the manner in which a person was murdered made her sick to her stomach.

It made her want to help Samantha and the rest of the victims more than ever.

"I don't think anyone's linked the deaths so far," James added.

"Are you saying Abrams didn't crack the case?" Lily asked.

"I'm saying there's newer technology these days that can help link those cases with this one—hopefully."

"All right, how else can I help?"

"I think I've got it from here."

She gave him a cold stare.

"I'll let you know, I promise, when I get a lead or have anywhere to go in this case. I think we're done here. Shall we?"

Lily scanned Samantha's pale, lifeless body. There had to be more she could do.

Consulting her for mortuary knowledge might be somewhat helpful for the case, but she had so much more to offer if James would let her get involved.

"Dr. Elliot, will you lift her shoulder again? I want to see the tattoo."

"Certainly." He obliged.

Lily pulled out her phone. "I'm taking a photo of the symbol anyway. You never know who might recognize something."

"Be careful who you talk to out there. Not everyone wants to help."

"I heard you, Detective." She tried to contain her sarcasm in front of Dr. Elliot but clearly had failed. "Soon, you'll be begging me to help with every case."

"I somehow doubt that."

"We'll see."

After they went their separate ways, Lily hit the ground running. A killer was on the loose, targeting females, carving symbols into their skin, then strangling them. She felt compelled to help solve this terrible case, even if James worried himself sick about her involvement.

To think this had been going on under her nose while she had been taking care of some of these victims. She'd assumed law enforcement had handled those cases, but she had to admit it was naive to assume every criminal case she'd come across had been cracked. Still, this felt like the one she had to solve. All the girls were in their twenties, which meant she needed to go wherever they might have also gone while they were still alive. The killer would've also been in those places hanging out, ready to pounce.

The first place Lily decided to visit again was

Gina's Beauty Bazaar. A mecca for beauty enthusiasts, the store attracted the young and hip. Gina Giordani had her own special flair. Never one to fall in with the crowd, she liked to sport a different hair color on a weekly basis to keep things interesting. Today, in the back office of the store, Lily's eyes skimmed over the pink ends of Gina's hair. She appreciated the bravado.

"Have you ever seen a symbol like this anywhere?"

Gina brought Lily's phone closer. "A lightning bolt? Looks like an amateur tattoo job."

"It was an amateur job, but we think the person who did it also killed her. There have been several other women murdered in the same way, with the same tattoo."

Gina's face barely changed.

Based on the rumor mill, Lily knew her past to be colorful. Gang rivalry and violent warfare had tainted most of her life, but she had never publicly spoken of any of it to Lily.

Gina took a deep breath. Her long, red-acrylic tips clicked as she turned the phone to different angles. Her long false lashes mesmerized Lily as she studied the image a little while longer.

She gave the phone back to Lily. "I haven't seen this particular symbol before. That's some pretty sick stuff, though. Reminds me of the time when I lived in the City. We had this guy going around stabbing people, would carve satanic symbols onto their faces." She traced her long red fingernail along her cheek. "That guy shot himself before the cops got him. That's the problem with these gangs. They'd rather die than get caught." She pointed a red talon at Lily. "I'll bet you've seen some interesting things in your work."

"I have, but I've never had to focus on the killer. I get enough information to restore the deceased back to some semblance of normal but not to see them get justice. This is all new to me."

Gina shook her head. "I can't talk about my past, but my advice to you is to stay out of it, especially if it's gang related. I've been living clean and simple for years now, and it's the best decision I've made."

"You're right about that," Lily agreed. "It's been an eventful couple of weeks, but I seem to have fallen into the crime world."

Gina tapped her nails on the desk and winked at Lily. "I don't envy you. Nobody bothers me here in my store, and that's the way I like it."

"You're sure you haven't noticed anyone with this tattoo or heard anything about it?"

"No, believe it or not, it's pretty cookie-cutter here these days."

"Where else could I find out more about this tattoo or the person who carved it?"

"Have you tried Old Town Bar? That would be my next stop if I were you. I'm in there all the time. There's always someone young enough to know your victim, and that bar tolerates the runaways and outcasts."

"That's a good idea." Energized by the prospect of a new plan, Lily stood up to leave.

"Lily?" Gina called as Lily stepped out the door.

Lily turned. "Yes?"

"Be careful out there. If you need anything, call."

Lily smiled as she slipped out. She had no doubt if she were in trouble, Gina would know who to call. And she certainly might need to.

****

A serial killer targeting females. That's all he needed. The chances of catching this killer were already so slim. Even the famous Don Abrams never caught the guy. What would make a difference this time?

James rubbed his tired eyes. His mind kept jumping back and forth between the case and Lily. Keeping her off the case would not be easy, particularly when her enthusiasm as she took a picture of the tattoo practically shouted. Plus, it made him grumpy. He couldn't contain his instincts, but he had promised he would try.

"You're wasting your time on that case." Abrams slid into James's office with a coffee mug hanging from his fingers." Every one of those girls was a runaway for some reason or other, so tracking down family was almost impossible. If or when I did find someone, they didn't care."

"Doesn't mean they don't deserve justice," James grumbled—because he felt like it.

"It is odd this guy suddenly came back after five years."

"You think it's the same guy?"

"If it's not, he's a copycat. Looks to be the exact same circumstance. The symbol shows no variance whatsoever. It's got to be the same guy." Abrams smirked. "What does Lily think?"

"She said she had seen those symbols before but not recently. She thought they were ordinary tattoos."

"Is she going to take the lead on this one? Maybe I'll stop by the Reynolds place to offer her the lead investigator role."

"You're hilarious. If I need her input, I know

where to find her."

"I doubt she'll let that happen." He took a sip of his coffee. "She's probably out interviewing anyone she can find in the East Borough neighborhood as we speak."

"Okay, you made your point. I can't tell her what to do. She's smart enough to know what's dangerous."

"Smart enough to go into the eye of the storm."

"I thought you wanted her help."

"I think she has good instincts. Whether or not that leads to trouble for her is your problem, not mine."

"You can really be a cold-hearted bastard sometimes."

"That's why I've lasted as long as I have."

"Get his legs!"

Shouting could be heard coming from the entrance of the station. Abrams leaned his body out of the office to get a better look. His expression showed little to no concern.

James stood up. "Anyone need help?"

Abrams stepped back into the office. "Nah, Big John's got it under control."

James needed to change the subject. "How's Shanna doing?"

"Recovered but traumatized. She's stopped drinking coffee, for life."

"Understandable. And she trusts Chris Tuchman to work at the funeral home and not conspire with Tina Collins?"

"Tina confessed to everything for a lesser charge. She maintained his innocence. And anyway, wasn't it your girlfriend who made the decision to hire him?"

"You said yourself she has good instincts. Do I

completely trust Chris Tuchman? No, but he also hasn't given us a reason not to."

"Innocent until proven guilty?"

"Guess so."

"I would keep an eye on him," Abrams said as he took another long noisy gulp of his coffee.

"Can't you do that? I've got a serial killer to work out. No leads. And a girlfriend to keep safe."

"Now that you mention it, maybe I will stop by the Reynolds place to check on things. Shanna likes it when I drop by unannounced."

"Are you sure about that?"

"No, but I'll take my chances. I do have one tip for you on the tattoo killer."

"What would that be?"

"Witnesses in the neighborhoods where the girls were taken said they heard the sound of a motorcycle."

"So the guy drives a motorcycle? Did anyone ID the bike?"

"No, no one has ever seen it. There's a motorcycle shop in Parkview, but their records didn't point to anyone suspicious in the area. He might be living in a different town, but all the murders were here."

"So should I interview every person in Manorview who has a registered motorcycle?"

"Wouldn't take that long. Lily would be perfect for the job."

James returned a cold stare. "I'm not sure that's the best use of her time. Remember, she's still running a business. I'll include her when her role is better defined."

"If it were up to you, it would never be defined."

"Not true. She's already helped with this case.

She's seen some of the other victims at the funeral home. The ones who ran away from decent families."

"Well, if Lily's not going door to door, I guess you will. Have fun. See you a lot later." Abrams waved and left the office.

"Thanks a lot," James grumbled to himself. Protecting Lily was more work than he'd anticipated. But it was necessary, very necessary. He holstered his gun before putting on his jacket and walked out of his office. The list of registered motorcycle owners was long but chasing down tedious leads was something he was used to doing. Even though he recognized it was the footwork that usually led to an arrest, he didn't have to like it.

Chapter Eighteen

Old Town Bar had a distinct smell. It made Lily think of unwashed carpet that had soaked up every spill since the bar opened its doors thirty years ago. Foul odors didn't seem to bother the regulars who sat in the corner booths, sipping hard liquor all day.

Nor did they seem to bother the more youthful Saturday night crowd. That's who Lily wanted to talk to—anyone Zachary's age. Twenty-somethings who may have seen the victims or the symbol somewhere.

The question now was how to approach them. Everyone in town knew who Lily Reynolds was and what she did for a living. Some thought what she did was kind of creepy, sometimes even calling her Lilith or Lilydeath. Par for the course. The mortuary field wasn't for everyone. Did the name-calling hurt her feelings? Somewhat. But since she loved her job, she'd chosen to ignore it and move on.

She eyed the crowd—mostly men—nearest to the bar. She decided to use that to her advantage and start there. She picked out a taller fellow who seemed to be the most popular, figuring he'd be the best at knowing what the kids were up to these days.

She pushed her way through the crowd, hoping her smile would open up the conversation gates. Her target did take notice of the only redhead in a sea of brunettes. In this case, her unique coloring worked to her advantage—a concept that rarely happened.

"Having a nice time?" Lily shouted at him through the noise.

He returned a sloppy grin. "Better now."

"You look like a smart guy. Mind if I ask you some questions?"

"Sure." He nodded enthusiastically, like a dog waiting for a treat.

"Have you ever seen this before?" Lily turned her phone around, showing him the photo of Samantha Riley's tattoo."

He gave Lily the once-over before looking at the lightning bolt symbol.

"Aren't you Zachary Reynolds's sister?" he asked, leaning in a bit too close to her and disregarding her question. His disheveled hair reminded her of her brother's hair first thing in the morning.

She smelled the beer on his breath, realizing quickly that he might not be as helpful as she'd first thought. "Yes, but have you seen this symbol?"

"Is that what's on your back? I hate to tell you, but they didn't do such a hot job. You should get your money back."

Lily rolled her eyes. Nope, this wasn't as easy as she thought.

"I can take a quick look at your back for you. I'm sure it looks better in person."

"No, thanks."

His finger made a lazy stroke up her arm. "Or I can show you where to get good tattoos real cheap."

"Hey, Lily? Is that you?" Her brother stepped in between her and her new friend.

"Zachary, I'm so glad to see you. I *really* need to

talk to you in private," she told him, relieved by the interruption.

He took one look at the swaying guy next to them, then grabbed her arm. They walked away from the center bar to escape the crowd. "Who was that guy?"

Even though they'd walked away from the group, Lily had to practically shout at Zach through the loud music. "I have no idea. You know I wouldn't normally be here if I didn't have a good reason."

"True. So what's the reason?"

"The Manorview Police have had an unsolved case for maybe five years. The killer struck again, basically picking up where he left off. He tattoos this symbol on his victims's backs." She showed him the picture. "Have you seen this anywhere or know anyone who might have seen it before?"

Zachary stared at the phone for quite some time. "Is that the victim?"

"Yes, that's Samantha Riley."

"How'd she die?"

"She was strangled."

"Cool."

"You see this stuff all the time, Zach. It's *not* cool."

"Yeah, but this is different. I'm never involved in the criminal side of things."

"Yes, you are involved. You seem to like being on the other side of the law—committing crimes."

"That's not what I meant."

Lily was beginning to think he may have had too much to drink himself. Loud laughing coming from the bar distracted her while Zachary went back to staring at the photo.

Lily sighed. She wanted to yank the phone away from him.

"I have seen this," he finally responded.

"Where?"

"You can't get mad if I tell you."

"That's never a good start."

"Promise me you won't get mad."

Lily stared at his angelic eyes framed by fiery locks. She was beginning to understand why redheads were never to be trusted. "I promise."

"I saw it on a guy's hand at a biker bar in East Borough."

Appalled at his stupidity, she yelped, "You went to a biker bar in East Borough? And you didn't get the crap kicked out of you?"

"I went with my buddy Jackson. He's pretty well respected there. I went to see what all the fuss was about."

"Have you ever heard of the expression curiosity killed the cat?"

"Nothing bad happened. It's a cool place as long as you know the right people."

"You saw the symbol tattooed on a guy's hand?"

"Yeah."

"Was he a regular there?"

"I think so. He was there both times that I went."

Her eyes widened. "You went twice?"

The sound of shattering glass made them both look toward the bar. The crowd had fanned out a bit toward them, but Lily couldn't really see who'd dropped the glass. She hoped a fight wouldn't break out.

"The biker bar is an interesting place."

Lily sighed again. It was like talking to a child.

"What did he look like?"

"Thick beard. Dark sunglasses. Red-and-white bandana around his head. Kind of beefy."

"And you're sure you saw this exact symbol on his hand?"

"I'm positive. It's on his right hand. The one he used to drink his beers."

"I need to go there."

"You can't go there, Lily. You'd be fresh meat. What if he wants to target you?"

"I'm not his type. He goes for the misfit type. Plus, you'll come with me. Bring that Jackson person, too. I'd like to think being a redhead has bought me a natural repellent."

"That won't be much help in that bar."

"In any case, I need to help solve this murder, and you're coming with me. I can't promise we won't get into trouble. We'll do our best not to piss anyone off."

"Why can't we just have James go in and take the risk? He'll have backup."

"I want to do this myself."

"To prove a point?"

"I want justice for Samantha Riley. But you can't tell Shanna. She'd lose her mind. Especially after what happened with Simon and the formaldehyde. She wouldn't want us to take any risks."

"She'd go nuts if she found out."

"So don't tell her. This isn't supposed to be fun, Zach. I'm only taking you to point out our guy and to have Jackson come along to appease the natives."

"All right, I get the picture."

"In fact, you should stay out of everyone's way," she said to reinforce things.

"I got it. I got it. I don't exist."

"Precisely, for your own good. I'm getting out of here. The crowd's getting rowdy, and I have no tolerance in my old age."

His eyes lit up. "When we catch this guy, can I come work with you and James on the crime circuit?"

"That would be a solid *no*."

"You're no fun."

"Never was. Never will be."

Lily went home that night with a lot on her mind. She'd gotten her brother involved, which hadn't been the best decision she'd ever made. But he had been the key to moving the case forward. Without Zachary, she had nothing. She'd still be at Old Town Bar interviewing drunks and possibly getting her ass squeezed as she moved through the crowd. She laid her head on the kitchen counter. The cold granite cooled her pounding head. Not her finest moment.

"What are you up to?" Shanna walked into the kitchen, grabbing a bottle of water from the fridge. "Want one?"

"No, thanks."

Shanna pulled up a barstool next to Lily. "You look stressed."

"Tired."

"Is James working you too hard?"

Lily heard the crackle of plastic as Shanna opened the bottle and took a sip. "No."

"You're hiding something. Don't you think I know you? Better than you do sometimes."

Lily lifted her head to look at Shanna's silvery-green eyes. The lines around them gave her an elegant and wise appearance. She'd lost some weight while she was in the hospital, but she'd been saying it was the best diet she'd ever had. That was Shanna. She had a talent for giving everything a positive spin.

"I'm involved in a case, but I can't tell you the details."

"Doesn't sound promising. Is it safe?"

"Not really."

Shanna nodded. "I thought not. Zachary's near-death experience and my poisoning don't change anything?"

"I can't explain it. I think I can help the victims, and I feel like I need to."

"And this isn't James pushing you?"

"If anything, he wants me off the case."

"If you go out on your own, he won't be able to protect you."

"I know that."

"Mom and Dad used to call you stubborn for a reason."

"Maybe. But I was never a troublemaker like Zachary. In fact, I think they would be proud of me, and I want you to be too."

Shanna smiled. "I am, and I'm certain they would be very proud of you." She rubbed Lily's back as she always did during troubling times. "Doesn't mean you should risk your life for approval. Mom and Dad would be proud that you've helped keep their business afloat. That should be all you need."

"I'm not seeking approval. I know they would be proud, regardless. Not going to lie, I do wonder what Dad would have to say about my new interest."

"He would've told you to cut it out because he would want you to be safe, but behind your back, he would've been smiling with pride."

As Lily's body relaxed, a grin appeared on her face. The idea that her dad might be looking down on her with pride made her day. Her mind cleared with renewed purpose. She'd almost lost her way, but Shanna had helped turn everything around.

"Thank you."

"You're welcome. Come on. Let's go to bed. Whatever you're stressing about can wait until morning."

"Yes, Mom."

"Don't forget it."

****

James put his head down on the desk. His eyes were blurry from staring at the blank screen in front of him. Fourteen hours had elapsed, and he'd gotten nowhere on the lightning bolt case. The motorcycle lead had not panned out. Sixty interviews in one day, and nothing. Abrams had been right about it all along. James had no leads, no suspects, and no witnesses.

He'd rarely been assigned a cold case file during his career. When it was, he remembered feeling as awful as he felt now. Useless was a better word. He'd looked at his phone numerous times, almost giving in and calling Lily for help, but the old demons stopped him from doing so. Dragging her into a violent crime where the killer would probably love to tattoo his ridiculous symbol on her back was not in the cards. A shudder went through him. No, feeling useless was infinitely better than getting her into trouble. He would have to work longer hours and think outside the box. Something had to come up.

Officer Leary poked his head in the door. "Hey,

Detective. We just got a call from a bartender out in East Borough. He's got a brawl going on between some of the locals—a young woman and her boyfriend. I thought I'd let you know since you've been working on that case with young female victims."

"Thanks, Dan. I'll look into it." Maybe this was the break he needed. "What's the name of the bar?"

"Metal Horse."

James froze. "What did you say?"

"The bar. It's called Metal Horse."

"Thanks." He needed to be sure he'd heard correctly. The last time Metal Horse came up was when he'd investigated Michael Ronan. He'd even gone there to look around but didn't see anything suspicious. He had to concede that he might have overlooked something.

James put on his holster and rushed off to his car. As he thought about it more, a biker bar sounded like the perfect link to Abrams's motorcycle theory, but it also was the last place he wanted to start trouble. The first time he'd gone there, he'd slid in and out, trying to remain undetected. He knew the patrons all had guns on them. His buddies Patrick Stern and Joe Richter might have been helpful for backup, but they were both on another case. He'd need to tread lightly if he didn't want to get himself killed.

A speedy but controlled drive over to the bar made James even more excited and nervous as he got closer. Would he finally catch the killer? Would this be the case that made him famous, like Abrams? He fantasized about the possibilities. This could be the break his career needed.

Every make and model of motorcycle lined the

driveway leading up to the entrance. James heard shouting and loud cheers before he'd even reached the crowd. As his car approached the entrance, he slowed to a stop. A group of bikers clustered outside the front entrance. The question was, did he want to intervene in a crowd full of huge biker dudes who were probably better armed than him?

James weighed his options. He could get out now, save his skin but enjoy countless sleepless nights, wondering if he's let the killer get away or take a chance the killer was inside and catch him. As much as his training had drilled caution into him for these types of decisions, he already knew what he had to do.

He stepped out of his unmarked vehicle and looked for a gap in the crowd to get a better look at what was going on. A large guy stood in the center of the ring. Mildly panting, he stared down at his victim laying on the ground a few feet ahead of him. James craned his neck around the broad shoulders in front of him to get a look at the one on the ground. His gut clenched, and he almost stopped breathing when he spotted red hair. *What was Zachary doing here?*

His heart thumped against his chest. *If Zachary was here, did that mean Lily was close by?* James whipped his head around, frantically looking around at the biker crowd. He needed to look for Lily, but he also needed to stop this fight.

James grabbed his police badge from his inside coat pocket and held it up. "All right, that's enough. Everyone back inside, except you." He pointed at the biker in the center with the red-and-white bandana. "Don't move," he told the biker as he knelt down to check on Zachary. He had a couple of black eyes, but he would live.

"Kid comes in here with his sister accusing me of killing people—"

Anger pulsed through his body. James pulled his gun out and pointed it at the biker. "Where is she?"

The biker put up both hands but smiled at James's reaction. "Not my type."

James gritted his teeth. "Where is she?"

"Inside."

James didn't wait to hear more. He rushed into the bar looking for Lily. He couldn't believe she'd taken this risk—that is, he could, but he hated it.

Inside, wooden paneling covered almost every inch of the bar. The multitude of leather jackets gave the air a musty scent. James surveyed the room, hoping to get a glimpse of red hair, but all he got was more of the same. Big biker dudes, some wearing bandanas, some wearing sunglasses, all holding cans of beer. James walked down the corridor leading to the bathrooms. If Lily was here, he was going to find her.

No lights came from the kitchen. At this time of night, it should be bustling with bar orders. James kept his gun pointed in front of him as he inched toward the swinging doors. He heard nothing on the other side of the doors. Maybe he was wrong. Maybe they didn't serve food, and Lily had been taken somewhere else. He shook his head. No, he wouldn't let his mind go down that road. She was here, and he would find her.

Smashing through the doors, he pointed his gun at the dark space ahead of him. The main kitchen space was clear. Large steel appliances lined the walls as he walked past a spotless center island. The door on the left side of the kitchen caught his eye. He stepped closer to it, hoping to hear voices. Hearing nothing, he grabbed the doorknob anyway and swung it open, keeping his gun pointed ahead.

Lily and her captor sat crouched on the floor. His hand was over her mouth while the other held a knife to her throat. Lily's eyes were filled with the kind of fear he never wanted to see.

"Let go of her. The bullet will hit you long before you even think about using the knife."

"Lester told me to keep her hidden here while he dealt with her brother. I'm only doing what I was told."

"I already talked with Lester. He's coming with me, and so are you. I suggest you let go of her. I have really good aim."

Her captor's bloodshot eyes darted back and forth as he considered his options. James knew this guy didn't have the guts. Hiding in the pantry was one clue, but the tremor in his chin sealed the deal.

"Let. Her. Go."

Another second and his arms loosened their grip on Lily. His arms went up, and she scrambled out of the pantry.

"Get up. Let's go." James corralled her captor toward the outside where he hoped Lester hadn't decided to skip town. His eyes skimmed over Lily. He saw she hadn't been hurt. She followed closely behind them.

Outside, Abrams stood next to a patrol car with Lester inside and Zachary leaning up against the side door. Besides looking like the loser in a boxing match, he didn't seem to need an ambulance.

"Get in," James told Lily's captor.

He went willingly.

James turned to Lily. He embraced her. Tightly. "Are you all right?" It wasn't the time to question her. He knew why she'd come here, and he wished she hadn't, but he was satisfied that nothing bad had happened to her.

"I'm fine. I wanted to get him. I had to get him."

James breathed in the lavender shampoo she used in her hair. "I know you did."

"Next time, I'll be armed."

"Is that right?" Her comment didn't make him feel better. But this was not the place to argue.

She gave a coy smile that melted away his fears. "Thanks for coming."

"No problem. Apparently, this is our new norm."

"Guess so. How's Zachary?"

"Beat up."

"I can see that."

"He'll live."

"How'd you know to come here?" James asked Abrams. His arm went around Lily's neck.

"Shanna. You know she can't keep a secret."

Lily turned toward Zachary. "We agreed we wouldn't tell her."

"Yeah, I know, but I thought someone else should know where we were in case things went badly."

"And they did...go badly," James added.

"I'm sorry I told her after we agreed not to, but I'm sure glad I did."

"So am I. It's okay, Zachary." James patted his shoulder. "You did the right thing."

"I'm sorry, Zach," Lily began. "It was all my idea. I thought we could identify the killer and leave without bothering anyone. But when Zachary saw the symbol on Lester's hand, I couldn't help myself. I wanted to tell him we were coming for him. I had such rage for what he'd done that I couldn't walk away."

"And what was the plan exactly? Tell a killer off and walk away?" James couldn't help himself. She'd made such a rash and careless decision that almost cost her life.

She gave him a cold stare.

"She solved a five-year-old cold case with seasoned detectives on the trail. She strolls in after a few days and solves it," Abrams added. "That's pretty impressive."

"I couldn't have done it without Zachary."

"Makes sense. You two are related," Abrams said.

"It was a group effort." Lily smiled awkwardly.

"Yes, a group effort. You run into danger, and I save you," James added.

"Get over it, James. She's part of the team now. You need a better strategy and, most importantly, you need to work together," Abrams said.

"Get over it? You were the one who kept saying she murdered Ronan. Now you're on her team?"

"Yup. That's right. I already apologized for that. Moving on."

"You're trying to bust my balls for solving the Tina case before you could."

"That too."

"I'm trying to keep her safe. I'd appreciate it if you'd stop egging her on."

"Not a chance."

"Abrams is right. Stop trying to throw me off the case. You'll see that if we cooperate, there won't be any surprises. And the best and most important part is we solved the case," Lily chimed in.

"And *you* solved the case," Abrams said.

"Details."

"Doesn't feel so nice, does it, James?" Abrams asked.

"What?"

Abrams winked at him. "Getting your case ripped out from under you."

James gave him a side-glance. "Point taken."

Chapter Nineteen

Lily tugged at the blindfold covering her eyes. "I can't see a thing."

"Nah-ah, we talked about this. I know relinquishing control is hard for you, but I promise the reward is worth it." James pulled her hand as he led her to a secret location. "I'll give you a hint. You've been here before."

She heard the sound of a door opening. "That's not a good hint."

"I didn't say it was a *good* hint. But you're going to be very pleased with me in the end."

Lily smiled. She'd never been surprised with anything in her life—let alone walking around blindfolded. James was right. Relinquishing control, in general, wasn't easy for her, but relinquishing control to *him* could be. He led her inside a drafty building with no carpeting. She knew that because her kitten heels clip-clopped with every step. She hoped he wasn't showing her another body in the morgue. Even though she appreciated the encouragement, she had less gruesome aspirations for their relationship.

"All right, here we are. Your new favorite place."

She felt him release the knot behind her head.

"Ta-da!" He pulled the blindfold away like a magician revealing his trick. "Your very own personal detective space."

The sudden brightness made Lily's eyes squint. When her vision returned to normal, she saw in front of her a brand-new wooden desk with a white laptop, a cup full of pens, and a bouquet of red roses in the center.

"This is for me?" Lily ran her hand along the smooth surface of the desk and eyed the crimson petals reaching out in full bloom.

"This is the best I could do for an unofficial consultant. Abrams contacted the higher-ups for a special favor. But I really had no choice. You have fully infiltrated my space. We can't both work out of my desk space. It would get too messy."

"You're only a few feet away. I can bother you as much as I want to. How did you know roses were my favorite?"

"It seemed obvious. Elegant. Fragrant. Beautiful. The perfect description of you."

Lily reached her hands around his neck. The blue in his eyes lit up the room. She arched up to meet his lips. He reciprocated and pressed his body into hers. She savored the moment between them. His acceptance of her as his equal and not his damsel in distress pleased her almost as much as the kiss.

He slowly pulled away. "I may never get any work done ever again, but this was my best idea yet."

"I don't disagree. Speaking of work, what happened to Lester, our tattoo artist?"

"Not your best transition, but I know you can't help yourself. Is this the way it will be? Me, trying to romance you, but you always talking about work?"

"No, but Lester got to me in ways that Tina and Simon didn't. Tina had an old vendetta she'd been holding onto all her life. None of which had anything to do with me. Simon idolized her. He wanted to have his own funeral home and thought the only way he could get that was to get rid of his competition. But what about Lester? What's his deal? Why was he killing those young girls? I want to know."

"Then I have another surprise for you."

"Oh, really?" She eyed him suspiciously.

"He's here. Locked up in a private cell all to himself before he goes in front of the judge. You want to ask him yourself? I can't promise the judge will allow the conversation as evidence, but I can do my own interrogation as well."

"Well, you've certainly changed your tune. You went from shutting me out from any investigations to handing me over to the killer himself."

"I wouldn't say I've handed you over to him. He's behind bars. I'm pretty confident he's not going to hurt you or anyone."

"What if he says something that scars me for life?"

"I'm confident you won't be affected. You're too smart for that."

"Progress." Lily smiled at the idea. He appeared to be giving her everything she wanted. Would it last? She couldn't be sure. "Where is he?"

"Cell three."

She noticed he didn't make any move to go with her. That made her suspicious. Was this his attempt at reverse psychology? He would let her go in front of a monster, and she would be so traumatized she'd never want to be involved in criminal investigation ever again? But this was what she wanted. Wasn't it? She didn't want him to think she had any trepidation about speaking to Lester. It would undermine her entire point.

"Great. See you in a bit," she told him.

"By the way, it would be nice if you found out the connection between Lester and Michael Ronan while you're there."

"Why would there be a connection?"

"Ronan also used to hang out at Metal Horse. At the time of his death, I didn't find anything suspicious there, but I doubt it's a coincidence. I wonder if Ronan also had something to do with the tattoo murders. See you soon," he said, staring down at his paperwork. "Oh, and take this with you." He placed his mini cassette recorder at the end of his desk.

She picked it up without looking at him. She didn't let him see her reaction to the newest bomb he threw at her. She walked out of the office a bit uneasy. Had she expected to be escorted? *Maybe.* But she knew that seemed silly.

Get a grip, Lily. This is what you wanted.

And now a possible connection to Ronan. Had he also been part of the sadistic game Lester played? Lily doubted Tina or even Sarah had known about this sick and twisted side of him. This was on a whole new level.

Down the corridor toward the holding cells, she walked until she approached the guard station. Jimmy sat at his post, watching his shows.

"Lily, nice to see you. What can I do for you?"

"I'm here to see cell three."

Jimmy didn't answer right away. He seemed confused by her request.

"I would talk to him through the bars if I were you. Might get a little crowded inside the cell with him."

She smiled. The urge to protect did not stop with James. "I'm not planning on going inside the cell. I wanted to speak with him, though."

"Be my guest. He's the only one here at the moment. If you need anything, just holler, or if you change your mind and want to watch *Simply Me*, I wouldn't mind starting the whole series over again. It's that good."

Lily laughed. "Thanks, Jimmy. If I change my mind, I'm heading right back over here."

"Good luck."

The hallway leading down to cell three gave her the creeps. Once you got past the guard station, silence prevailed. She wished she hadn't worn heels that were basically announcing her approach. She had to be strong. The chills down her back meant nothing compared to passing the test James had put forth. Cells one and two were empty, leaving her completely alone with a killer.

Before she saw inside cell three, she took one more deep breath and let the anger she held inside for his crimes replace her fear.

"I know you're there. I heard your footsteps," Lester's scratchy, deep voice announced before she'd come into his view.

"I'm not trying to surprise you." She finally got to see him slouched over in one corner of the concrete cell. The red-and-white bandana remained tied to his head. He seemed to be staring down at his right hand, stroking his tattoo.

"You're lucky I didn't tell Bob to just slit your throat and throw you in the river. He would've done anything I told him."

"And why didn't you? I didn't fit your profile? I wasn't worthy enough?"

"You have nothing on me. You have assault."

"Kidnapping."

"Hard to prove. You went to Metal Horse on your own."

"I did. I wanted to meet you. I wanted to meet the man who branded young women like cattle. But what I haven't figured out is if you were bothering to tattoo them out of some narcissistic fantasy or if it was a way to control them even in their death."

"Lady, I've seen all the psychiatrists. It means nothing to me."

"Does that mean you've had a hard life?"

He chuckled and looked up at her. "You have no idea. Someone with your charmed life wouldn't be able to comprehend a guy like me."

"Why not? I'm a mortician. Death is what I do."

He stared at her as if processing what she'd said. "We're not so different then. Sick puppies. Why do you like death?"

Lily breathed in as she thought about his question. "I believe what I do brings peace. I remember as a teenager my grandmother died alone in her apartment. Someone in the building dropped a lit cigarette, and the whole place went up in flames. She needed a walker to get around and didn't make it out in time. Her body had burned in such high heat, only fragments of bone survived. She couldn't get a proper burial. To me, she never got the final resting peace she deserved. Instead, her last day on this Earth was painful and violent. I wanted to spend the rest of my life bringing people peace."

"People die violently every day. There's nothing that you can do to stop it."

"And what do you bring? Chaos?"

"Chaos is powerful. Each of those girls was born from chaos and died that way. It was the right way."

"To be murdered?"

He stood up but stayed toward the back of the cell. "I did those girls a favor. I am the reaper for lost souls. You should be thanking me." He sat down and turned away from her.

She knew the anarchist in him wouldn't be able to resist a moment to preach.

"What about Michael Ronan?"

"He's dead, but I didn't kill him."

"I know that. Why is he associated with Metal Horse? I find it hard to believe he likes the atmosphere."

"Ronan had all the same beliefs I do. He may have hidden it under a day job and a clueless girlfriend, but he happened to be one of my faithful followers. Too bad he got involved with that crazy woman. He still would've been helping me find those losers."

"Good riddance to both of you."

She walked back to her office, sick to her stomach. Ronan had been part of the whole sick game, and they had no idea. It made her wonder about Tina. Had she known? Had Sarah known? She couldn't be happier it was over. As she got further away from Lester, her spirits lifted. She'd done what she'd been asked to do successfully. Not bad for a rookie. Lily passed Jimmy on the way.

"All set?"

"Absolutely. Thanks, Jimmy."

"No worries."

She realized the smile on her face as she entered the office would be borderline obnoxious, but it could not be contained.

"That good?"

She nodded. "That good."

"You're amazing. You know what that means, right?"

"He pays for his crimes and is off the streets?"

"It also means we didn't have to settle for a reduced sentence in exchange for a confession. I have a reputation for getting confessions, but you blew that out of the water. You're better than me."

Lily put her arms around him. She stared up at his glimmering blue eyes, knowing the answer before she asked the question. "Can you handle that?

"Definitely," he answered quickly. "Did you find out what Ronan had to do with it?"

"He was in on it. Seems as if Lester was the ringleader. But we'll never really know since Ronan can't speak for himself, and neither can the victims."

"Crazy world, but I'm glad you're in it." He leaned down and pressed his lips against hers. She let the softness of his lips take over her mind and body until she felt as if they were the only people who mattered.

Then she pulled away, feeling more at ease than she'd ever felt in her whole life. This felt good. This felt right. "Welcome to a new beginning for us and, most importantly, today marks the day we bring those girls some peace."

Chapter Twenty

Lily looked down at the long white veil gathered at her feet. So much had happened in the past year that culminated in this moment. Her marriage to James had surprised her. She knew she loved him, but she had not followed her own rules. Instead, she had followed her heart. When was the last time she'd done that? Once. After her parents's death, she'd fallen in love with the drummer in a band she'd met out one night. She'd begged Shanna to let her move to California for the summer. At first, Shanna stood firm, but Lily continued to hound her until she'd grown fed up with her. Needless to say, she'd gone out to California and had never felt freer. The relationship didn't last, and Lily returned to Manorview. But she didn't regret it. She'd taken a risk, followed her heart, and even if it didn't work out, she was glad she had the experience. Marrying James brought her to that place again. Free. Risky, but amazing.

"You look pensive," Shanna said, walking into the bride and groom's lounge with a tray containing two champagne glasses and small, sweet chocolate bites. "Where's your husband?"

"In the bathroom, fixing his bow tie."

Shanna put the tray down on the table. "Everything all right?"

"I was thinking about how I got here."

"That was a crazy time, growing up without parents."

"And look where you are now."

"I wouldn't be here without your patience and guidance after Mom and Dad died. So thank you."

"You're going to make me cry off my mascara. That poor girl who put it on worked so hard to make me look acceptable." Shanna twirled in her navy satin sheath.

"You never looked better."

"Neither has Zachary. The last time I saw him in black was at our parents's funeral—sorry, poor taste. I think he loved giving you away. Since we both give him a lot of crap all the time for being a hooligan, I think it made him feel important and grown up."

"Agreed. He had quite a grin on his face afterward."

"And who knows—maybe Julie will catch the bouquet."

"That would be amazing."

"Buck up. You should be smiling the whole day. Less worrying, more smiling. You've earned the right to have the best day of your life and the best husband."

Lily smiled. "What about you? Any thoughts on wearing one of these one day?" She gathered up the white silk with her hands.

"Never say never. But Abrams may be too set in his ways."

"Never say never. I happen to know he's on the cusp of asking for your hand," James said, coming out of the bathroom.

"Ah, the groom. I brought you two some refreshments."

"You are so kind and looking mighty elegant," James added.

"Ditto. I will leave you two to enjoy each other's company. See you at the reception," Shanna said, slipping out of the couples's room.

James grabbed one of the champagne glasses and handed it to Lily.

She loved champagne. The bubbles. And how relaxed she felt after just one—not that drinking champagne happened all that often.

"You look beautiful. Stunning."

"You look as handsome as ever. I must say, I'm not sure how I got here."

"I'll tell you. From the day you laid your eyes on me, you were hooked." He couldn't keep a straight face.

Lily traced the lines around his eyes—her favorite part. His bright blue eyes, striking against the black tuxedo and slicked-back hair. Normally, she would've reacted with fire at his comment, but today the fire had gone out. Did that mean she had found her peaceful place?

"You're right. I was hooked, but not before you were instantly obsessed with me. You were the one following me around pretending I was a suspect. When all along, you were just stalking me."

"Not true. I'm a professional. I knew you couldn't possibly have done it, but you were closely tied to the person who did. Plus, getting involved in your world intrigued me."

"I don't believe you. I think in the beginning, you thought I may have killed Michael Ronan to save my creepy business. But that's okay. I've forgiven all of your past erroneous judgments. Especially since you worked past your issues to be with me." Lily grinned. "Let's make a toast." She raised her glass. "To us, for getting through our differences and finding in each other what really matters."

James raised his glass. "And to you, for trusting that I could get over my past and sticking with me through the hard times. You have my heart, and together we make an amazing team." He clicked his glass to hers, and they both took a sip.

Lily smiled. She relished the opportunity to give him a hard time. "Can I be the lead on the next case?"

"No, you don't actually work for the police force. You're a mortician and a great one at that."

"I know that, but you can't deny I've helped enormously. I think I can build a case on my own. Didn't I basically solve the tattoo case on my own?"

"No, you didn't. Yes, you went around asking the right people questions, and that got you in the right place, but without support, who knows what would've happened to you? When I got there, Zachary was on the floor with his face bashed in, and you were in a closet with a knife to your neck. I went there because a witness called the precinct, and Shanna was tipped off by Zachary." James's voice rose as frustration seeped in him. "If it had all been up to you, I don't think either of you would still be alive. You foolishly played with a serial killer and thought you would get out alive?"

"All right, all right. You clearly haven't had a chance to get this off your chest. You're right. I got too cocky. I hadn't had a real plan after I identified Lester as the killer. I promise I'll work on that. I'm sure I would've come up with something—"

"You would've been killed." James's nostrils flared. "It's this arrogant attitude that drives me crazy. That is not how an officer behaves. You don't strut up to a killer and expect that to go well. There are procedures in place. You can't do this alone." James took a step back, taking in a deep breath. "I'm sorry. That case really scared me."

Normally, calling her arrogant would provoke a fight that she would have no choice but to engage in. But she couldn't ignore the fact that he was right. She had acted in ways that put her own family's lives and herself at risk. "No, I'm sorry. You're right—I was careless and driven by my desire to solve the case."

"In order to make this work, we have to work as a team. This isn't a competition. We all want the same thing—to solve the case. But you're not a trained officer. You need backup in case things get aggressive—which they will." He stepped closer to her, grabbing her hand and squeezing it. "I want you to be safe. Above everything else, I don't want to lose you."

"You're right. I've been focusing on the wrong thing. I got caught up in discovering this new world to the point where I let everyone down—and the worst of all, I let you down. I promise from now on to work with you as a team because I don't want to lose you either. I love you."

He leaned in to brush her lips with his in the gentlest way possible.

Relief filled her body. She realized she wasn't the easiest to deal with, especially once she set her mind on something. She was never a troublemaker growing up. She didn't give Shanna a hard time, but she also never backed down from getting what she wanted. She hoped

James would continue to have patience and understanding.

A knock at their door brought them apart.

"Ready for your first dance, Mr. and Mrs. Rivers?" The wedding planner stood at the entrance, holding her clipboard against her stomach.

"Yes, we are," James answered. He took their glasses and set them on the table.

"There is one thing I haven't told you," Lily said as he took her hand.

"Whatever it is, it's too late now, Mrs. Rivers." He smiled.

That's why she loved him. He was in it with her until the end.

"I've decided something very important."

"What's that?"

"I've decided that I do, in fact, date cops."

He smiled. "I knew that all along."

A word about the author...

When Ana Diamond isn't writing about tough gals finding love in unexpected places, she's at work by day in the medical field. She writes romantic cozy mystery novels with feisty, strong women and alluring men who can't resist them. Her books are fast paced, entertaining, and heartfelt all at once.

Thank you for purchasing
this publication of The Wild Rose Press, Inc.

For questions or more information
contact us at
info@thewildrosepress.com.

The Wild Rose Press, Inc.
www.thewildrosepress.com